THE JIGSAW MAN

"a thriller with depth and wit and a ring of newly revealed truth that goes beyond cynical exposure . . . The twists and turns of the plot, all logical, all easy to follow are amazing."—Asheville, N.C., Citizen-Times.

"clever, witty . . . brilliant . . . The epilogue is bound to be a surprise even to the most avid of suspense and mystery readers."
—West Coast Review of Books

"the story moves intelligently, gracefully, crisply along with Miss Bennett pyramiding complications and building tension skillfully while she introduces a cast of well-etched, interesting characters. Her story has verve, wit, excitement and genuine toughness." —Buffalo Evening News

"Miss Bennett writes with a fast-moving sweep and with a flip humor that in no way diminishes the seriousness . . . There's a lot of ingenuity and originality here, and more suspense than you have encountered in a long time."
—Waco, Texas Tribune-Herald

"Compulsive reading."
—Cleveland Plain Dealer

About The Author

Dorothea Bennett lives in London with her husband, film director Terrence Young. Since leaving her native Ireland, she has gone fishing in Burma, pony riding in the Himalayas, houseboating in Kashmir, cameling in the Egyptian desert, flying in Persia, housekeeping in California, and idling in the Bahamas. She is the author of two earlier novels, *The Dry Taste of Fear* and *Under the Skin*.

The Jigsaw Man

Dorothea Bennett

WARNER BOOKS

A Warner Communications Company

Library of Congress Catalog Card Number: 75-38926

ISBN 0-446-89414-1

This Warner Books Edition is published by arrangement with Coward, McCann & Geoghegan, Inc.

Cover design by Gene Light

Cover art by Larry Noble

Warner Books, Inc., 75 Rockefeller Plaza, New York, N.Y. 10019

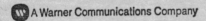 A Warner Communications Company

Printed in the United States of America

Not associated with Warner Press, Inc. of Anderson, Indiana

First Printing: July, 1977

10   9   8   7   6   5   4   3   2   1

TO

H.A.R. (Kim) Philby
Guy Burgess
Donald Maclean
Gordon Lonsdale
Peter & Helen Kroger
Klaus Fuchs
Dr. Alan Nunn May
George Blake
Harry Houghton
Rudolph Abel
John Vassall
. . . . . . all those not yet surfaced . . . . . .
&
My dear friends in the K.G.B.

THE
JIGSAW
MAN

Prologue

Philip Kimberly read his own obituary twenty-four days before Christmas.

Kimberly had answered his door reluctantly, only to stop the persistent knocking and to shout "Get out," but his fat friend Boris Medvedev pushed past him into the room. Following his fleshy rump, Philip automatically complained.

"It's Sunday, Boris. I don't want to appear inhospitable, old boy, but it is the Seventh Day. Even in Moscow. I have my praying to get through." Kimberly folded his hands devoutly. "Hail and Farewell, Mary."

Boris took a step closer to the gas stove.

"It is urgent, Philip, or I would not be here." He waved an envelope. "From the Top."

Though he liked to use his English with Kimberly, he now spoke Russian, triggering a small alarm in Philip's head. He pulled a sad mouth.

"Another ticking off, is it?" He folded defencelessly into a chair. "You read it, Roly-Poly. Read

9

it quietly. But let us have a small drink first." His patience suddenly wore thin. "And stop waving that letter like a fly-swatter!"

Boris's eyes drifted to where he knew the bottle was kept.

"Yes," he warned. "You will need it."

He dropped the envelope into Philip's lap and reached for the bottle. Philip recovered his calm and stretched his legs towards the fire. "And when does a man not need vodka? Pour!" he said.

"Read," Boris urged.

Philip fingered the envelope. Boris wiped and filled two glasses. He handed one to Philip. They toasted each other automatically.

"God bless Vod!"

Philip handed back the empty glass for a refill and picked up the letter. He tore the envelope and pulled out a newspaper galley-proof which had been set for publication.

"You must check it for mistakes, yes?"

Boris poured more vodka. Philip adjusted the proof for easy reading. Suddenly he pulled it to a closer focus.

"What is this!"

Boris glanced at him with a melancholy smile. "A death in the family," he said.

Kimberly's eyes raced down the column, his shocked brain registering only the salient facts:

> *MOSCOW, March 24 (Tass)—The death of Philip Kimberly was announced here today . . . death caused by aggravated cir-*

*rhosis of the liver . . . born London, 1912
. . . son of Sir Arthur Kimberly, Bart., K.C.
. . . mother, Lady Constance Kimberly . . .
came down from Christ Church College,
Oxford, 1929 . . . political analyst . . .
Spectator, New Statesman, 1935 to 1939
. . . served with distinction in British Intelligence during the war against the fascist,
imperialist beasts . . . married 1950 . . . a
daughter, Penelope, born 1952 . . . emi-
grated to Russia, 1964 . . .*

Philip crushed the obituary in his hand.

"So! They've decided on the chop, have they?
March 24. Nearly four months. Why the delay!"
Boris shrugged lazily with his left shoulder, offering consoling vodka. Philip jumped to his feet,
wrathfully knocking the glass from Boris's hand
to the floor. His face, latterly debauched and discontent, drew itself together like a wizened fist
for an ineffectual blow. His voice rose stridently:
"They can't treat *me* like some petty courier!
Petty currency for a swap of petty political pris-
oners or down the drain. I'm an important—an
international figure! I came to Russia only when
the bungling Burgess put me in the cart in England! I was Director of the Russian Desk in the
Foreign Office! I might even have been Prime
Minister by now, the Kremlin still kissing my
arse!"

Again Boris shrugged that lazy left shoulder.
"But, today, if you should go back to England,

they would not give you five years in the House of Commons: they would give you thirty years in Brixton Prison."

Philip grasped at the feeble straw hungrily: "Is *that* it? That's what they think? That I'm planning to—? Never! Who suggested it? Not I! Why, this is—is—Boris, Boris, what brought this about?"

Boris spread his hands and sighed with that Russian melancholy.

"Ah, Philip, Philip, my dear comrade. You know as well as I: you have been restless, discontent, a nuisance, and a drunken embarrassment for a long, long time. But it was finally last week that you killed yourself. Yes, at the dinner the Chairman gave for the Jugoslavs."

Philip Kimberly shook his head slowly from side to side, denying everything, the head still heavy with the memory of that unending hangover.

"No," he whispered. "No, no, no . . ."

"Yes," Boris said. "Yes, yes, *and* yes. When you kissed the President."

"But, Boris—it's absurd! Yes, I was drunk. But we were *all* drunk. For once in our benighted lives we were having a good time. And I was the life and soul of the party, God damn it! I was kissing my comrades. We always kiss our comrades!"

"But the President? Surely, not the President. And not on the lips!"

"A joke, Boris! What did it matter? There

12

were no ladies present. And the President even smiled!"

"I know, Philip," Boris said gravely." But that was before you peed on the table. In front of the Jugoslav Deputy-Prime Minister." Boris sighed deeply. *"You*—our star turn!"

"I passed out!"

"First you passed water, *then* you passed out."

Suddenly Boris began to laugh, half at his own wit and half at the horrific memory. He shook with mirth beyond his control. Happy tears sprang to his eyes and leaked onto his fat cheeks.

Philip tried to join him, tentatively at first, then happily, hopefully: it was a joke. The whole thing was a joke. The obituary—who'd thought of *that?* What a lark! And Philip got carried away on the waves of Boris's laughter: his relief was beyond bearing as Boris spluttered: "Like a —like a seaside donkey on the beach at Sochi! The full hot stream over everything!" He wiped his eyes, fought for control. "Oh, my friend, my friend, what a glorious end! You passed out and you didn't even button your fly. One of the guards rushed you with his gun: for a moment I thought he was going to shoot your prick to hell where it belonged! But no—all he did was zip you up and bow apologetically to the Jugoslav Deputy-Prime Minister!"

One hour and two bottles of vodka later, they came for Philip Kimberly. He was taken to a hospital a short distance north of Moscow. It was a building tightly folded in a forest which also embraced the Special School of the State Security Services, a little-known area tightly controlled by the K.G.B.

And now, on the operating table, Philip Kimberly groaned.

The second surgeon glanced at the anaesthetist. A nurse pressed forward. The anaesthetist slowly increased the rate of oxygen-flow. Philip Kimberly stopped groaning.

Presently the surgeon flung several kilos of solid white lard into the slop bucket. When he had finished stretching the skin back over the abdomen and cut the excess away, he clamped the long incision with a few metal clips.

"Suture," he said to his assistant. "Finest possible stitching. This fish is being prepared for some special table. See that he looks good enough to eat."

For the first time since the operation began, his eyes left his patient. He nodded a thank you to his staff and strode briskly to the scrub-room.

While the scrub-nurse removed his mask and gloves and overall, she managed, apparently inadvertently, to lightly caress his crotch. He favoured her with a broad wink as he sat down. The girl gave the bundle of soiled linen to an orderly who took it away.

As the scrub-nurse bent to remove the loose plastic boots, the surgeon slid his hand down the neck of her uniform and fondled her left breast.

He idly wondered who his patient was and why such trouble had been taken to remove the flesh of overindulgence, and in such secrecy. He would never know. He sighed. He began to seriously stroke the nurse's right breast.

Philip Kimberly emerged from the anaesthetic. His hands, still not completely under his control, wandered somewhat aimlessly in the direction of the pain. He wondered what the hell was hurting so much. He felt he had been sawn in half. The post-op drugs took over and gave him another two hours of dreamless sleep.

His second waking was worse, both physically and mentally. He remembered being taken to a hospital. He remembered fighting, although he knew it was useless to curse or shout or struggle. But, whatever was going to be done to him, he was determined to give them a tough time. He remembered Boris Medvedev grinning at him.

"Minor surgery," he had said.

Christ! Had they decided to relieve him of the offending organ which had, of its own volition it still seemed to him, urinated so generously on the damask of the President's table? Philip forgot his physical pain in the intense mental agony: those bastards would do anything!

This time, his hands obeyed the command of his head. They found what they were looking for. His prick was still there.

Philip Kimberly opened his eyes.

Boris Medvedev was still grinning at him from the bedside as though he had never moved.

"Minor surgery," he said again.

Philip blinked to clear his sight. This was obviously some kind of recurrent nightmare. But the physical pain was enough to assure him it was no dream. What had they done to him? His spirit coiled itself for one last strike. He tried to fling himself on Medvedev but all he managed was to raise his shoulders from the bed before falling back in agony. He let out a roar of pain and anger.

"What the hell have they done to me? Oh, Christ, it hurts! Bastards, bastards!"

"The pangs of your rebirth, Philip."

A nurse hurried into the room. She glanced enquiringly at Boris as she crossed swiftly to the bed.

"What's the trouble?"

"I am in pain, my good woman! In pain, I tell you! Get me a doctor!"

"Cosmetic surgery, comrade," she said blandly. "Surely you are prepared to suffer for such vanity?"

She swabbed his perspiring face efficiently with a warm, wet gauze-pad. Philip submitted, trying desperately to find sense in her words. Cosmetic surgery?

"What's she getting at, Boris?" He groaned. "Oh, God—get me some pills, a doctor, a drink. Boris, Boris!"

He heard the phrases slurring from his furred

mouth when he intended them to be crisp, authoritative and to be obeyed.

The nurse had her hand beneath his head, offering water from an invalid-cup. He gulped gratefully and greedily.

"Enough water for now. I will bring you pills."

She wiped his lips again and turned to Boris. She whispered something into his ear and left the room. Boris pulled up a hard chair close to the bed. He brought his head down to Philip and put a cautioning finger to his lips.

"Do not speak," he whispered. "It will be all right."

"Shit on that!" Philip rasped. Boris patted the bedcover. "And on that!"

Boris grinned again.

"That is my friend. A phoenix from the ashes. From the hulk that once used the President's table as a *pissoir* emerges a thing of beauty. Slender." Boris's hands described a shape in the air. "From the pampered belly of Philip Kimberly, four kilos of unwanted capitalistic blubber have been removed so that he can be reborn. It is bound to cause a slight stomach-ache."

The nurse came back into the room. Philip Kimberly felt his head spinning as she pressed two tablets into his mouth, offered a further sip of water, and left them.

"Yes, yes . . . " Boris was going on. "You are a very fortunate man, my friend."

Philip drifted off to sleep again.

That was the first operation.

Many weeks of great discomfort followed. But, over and above it all, was the agony of his forced withdrawal from alcohol, until at last he lost the craving. He was left numb and dispirited and, for the first time in his life, aware of the miasma of fear.

They altered the shape of his aristocratic nose, broadening the bridge and slightly flattening the tip. The cheekbones had been subtly raised, and the eyes given a Slavic slant. The puffy flesh of the face was removed, the sagging chinline lifted, the skin tightened everywhere.

When he was fit enough, he underwent progressive physical training with a professional athlete. He felt long-forgotten muscles come back to life. One day he floored the instructor with a sharp right hook.

The man danced with pleasure: "Good, good!"

Until then, Philip had adopted an overt lack of interest in what was being done to him. But inside, a mixture of anger, lurking fear, and intense curiosity fermented.

Now, tentatively, in the dark of the hospital room as his scars mended, he drew fingers over new contours and let his tongue explore the shape of his recapped front teeth.

Eventually he was taken out of doors to jog around a yard. He was urged to beat a tennis ball against a wall. He scented the air for change of season, but found no promise of spring or of anything at all. He resented the tailoring of his body. He missed the fleshy covering behind which he had lived and hid since he was young. People trusted a well-covered man, a good fellow who would indulge himself and did not fear to drink, a man fond of decent living. This slim, ever-hardening body was foreign to his soul. It made him feel vulnerable. He knew it could not accommodate the man within.

Finally came a day when after the barber had finished shaving him, the nurse brought in a hairdresser. He gave Philip a professional smile and complained petulantly about the lack of a looking-glass before he got to work. To begin with, he massaged Philip's scalp and examined the neck and ears for scars. Hs consulted a sheet of notes: he had been instructed what to look for and what to do.

He used a straightening lotion and trimmed the hair. He dyed it and shampooed it once again. It took a long time. Philip wondered yet again what he was being groomed for. This massive disguise must lead to a weighty purpose. But what? Boris Medvedev was still the only contact with his former life. Emotionally, Philip tried to persuade himself that the Russian was still his friend. Experience and reason, however, left him with the chill certainty that no officer at the core of the K.G.B. could have any loyalty outside the organisation. Philip knew it would be useless to ask Boris the name of the game. It was more than likely that Boris himself did not know. They played chess and discussed sport. Boris made flattering comments on the physical change in his friend. He had even made an abortive attempt to lose some of his own weight but, to Philip, he now seemed fatter than ever before.

When the hairdresser had finished, photographs were taken of his newly styled head before he was locked in alone again.

Boris Medvedev appeared on the morning after the hairdressing session. The nurse brought him in and they both laughed and admired the latest change.

As soon as the nurse had left them alone, Boris put his finger to his lips and handed Philip a small pocket mirror. The gesture of complicity gave Philip the first hope he had felt in months. Boris walked to the window and began an inane complaint against the weather. Philip looked first at Boris and then into the looking glass.

Instead of a debauched Englishman of sixty-two with a greying leonine head and large ears, he saw an interesting face—perhaps fortyish, a definite Slavic type. He stroked a sideburn and explored an ear pinned neatly and closely to his head. He glanced again at Boris and looked back to the strange reflection in the mirror. Boris took it from him and put it in his pocket just before the nurse returned.

"So," she said. "You are leaving us today."

Boris Medvedev drove Philip Kimberly back to the city along the Moskva River. Philip looked up towards the many cupolas, still clad in gold and silver. He stared at the lanterns and the slender tent-shaped pinnacles: a prodigious stage-decor painted against the vast background of sky. He glanced at Boris from the corners of his new Slav eyes.

"The second act?" he asked quietly.

Boris could no longer contain his good news.

"They are sending you back to England," he whispered, bouncing a little in his seat. "I am going with you. *England!*"

Kimberly's face remained cool and impassive. "Is that a treat or a threat?"

Boris looked pained. "I am going with you, Philip, because every man—even you—needs a friend."

Suddenly Philip smiled, a first attempt at smiling after a long time: a sad, tight smile showing his new square teeth. He laid a hand on Boris's knee.

"He does, indeed," he said softly. "Especially one who is a stranger even to himself."

Boris drove through the Spassky gates of the Kremlin to a remote part of that vast conglomeration of buildings.

They had not long to wait in a large reception room before the duty officer opened an upholstered leather door leading to a comparatively

21

small, functional office. A tall man in plainclothes stood beside a desk. He nodded a curt, official greeting.

Boris pulled himself to close attention.

Kimberly murmured, "Good afternoon."

The meeting in the Kremlin did not take long.

The tall man folded himself into the chair behind the desk and stared at Philip. He seemed satisfied.

"Yes. Remarkable. You will do." For what, Philip wondered again. "You have been given a new identity, a new persona," the tall man continued, "so that you can return to London. You will go as commercial attaché to our embassy there."

Philip's bland voice was softly mocking. "It is scarcely my field, sir. "

"An extremely important portfolio is missing."

Philip heard Boris shuffle his feet nervously and knew that now it was coming.

"It has been missing for ten years." The tall man stared sternly at Philip, eyes as flinty cold as a Moscow winter night. "Yes, since you defected to Russia ten years ago."

Whatever they had done to his exterior, Philip Kimberly was still the same man inside. His eyes met the Moscow winter calmly.

"And this concerns the commercial attaché?"

"The portfolio contains a record of every payment made to every one of our agents in the West since the early twenties. Names, dates, and signed receipts. Including payments made to yourself."

"I don't understand, sir. I have served the Party for forty years, since I was a young man at university. With great enthusiasm. I have served the Party better than most men."

"No one denies your usefulness in the past."

"I am glad to hear it—sir."

"It is your *future* I am talking about."

"And I am glad to hear there is *that*—sir."

"It depends on you. We have reason—*always* had reason—to believe you can restore to us this portfolio."

"I am afraid I have no knowledge of it—sir."

"It is our belief that, in the last hectic hours before you made your escape from England, you took it. You stole it. Your intention was always to bargain with it—if things became difficult for you. That day has come."

Philip used his new Slav smile.

"The day to bargain—comrade?"

Ignoring the remark, the tall man took a Russian passport from a drawer of the desk.

"In return for the portfolio, you have a new Russian diplomatic passport."

Philip stepped forward to take it. He opened it and looked at a photograph of his new face and new name. Sergei Kuzminsky. He noted that Kuzminsky was forty-two years old. He had a feeling that Sergei Kuzminsky would never reach forty-three.

"There are one million Swiss francs to your credit in a numbered account in Zurich," the tall man went on. "Comrade Medvedev has the details. He will accompany you to London to receive the portfolio. News of the death of Philip Kimberly reached London today. Your obituary will be published tomorrow. If, however, Comrade Kuzminsky fails to deliver the portfolio, he will not go to Zurich. He will be returned here to Moscow. And another obituary will be published."

Philip could see the hatred in the tall man's eyes. Nevertheless, he tried again with the cryptic Slavic smile. "I have no knowledge of any portfolio—comrade."

Once more, Boris scraped his feet uneasily. The tall man behind the desk rose.

"That is all," he said.

In the open, before they got back into the car, Boris pleaded with him. "They *know* you have it, Philip. They know you have it hidden somewhere in England. You would never have lasted this long if they didn't know you have it!" He spread his hands in despair. "Zurich. All that money. Think of it. A new life!"

Philip Kimberly looked at Boris for a moment, that small, melancholy smile on his lips.

Ah, Boris, Boris, he thought sadly, *you are the most profoundly boring man.*

He knew, and he knew Boris knew, that the moment he handed the portfolio to his friend, he

24

would be well and truly a dead man. His obituary would have been published only a few days too soon.

One

Harold Farquar flew to London from New York, arriving at Heathrow Airport on the morning of March 25.

His department had deemed it necessary to bring up-to-date their running-file on what Uncle Sam's current initial strategy would be if it became necessary for the U.S.A. to take up arms against the British. Farquar and his colleague, Paul Ives, had spent four months in America, probing gently at the periphery of the United States War College, a subtle think tank such as every major power kept permanently in session, devising and revising the pre-emptive strike against a former ally should such an action become categorically imperative.

The attack would have to be swift and decisive, a fait accompli before breakfast. The Establishment was well aware that the Western mind would respond unwillingly to vapourising friends of yesteryear. Old photographs of Dad in uniform, arms linked with pals from overseas, would bear emotional weight, creating not a slim Fifth Column to wrinkle out, but a vast army sluggish to draw blood.

The United States, in its magnificent isolation, would find its populace more difficult to manoeuver than Britain, France, and smaller powers who had the constant pinpricks of proximity to keep a healthy animosity not far under the skin.

War College is a very private place.

Farquar and Ives had soon established successful covers. Paul, an accomplished artist, had only to open his colour box and shop locally for canvases. Farquar fished. They rented a white, wooden house leaning over a lake outside the town sheltering the War College. It turned out as they expected: lakeside dwellers needed no parish pump to gather by for gossiping, and the weekenders were easygoing and hospitable.

Eventually they found the hairline crack they had been seeking: a hard man with a soft centre which Paul Ives tentatively explored. Farquar enjoyed a mild flirtation with his wife, a lady eager to lend tarragon and bunches of fennel. The three men and the woman settled down to gastronomic meals and serious week-end drinking.

It was Paul Ives who brought their mission to complete success. Farquar had sensed him growing tense and mysteriously remote. The following week-end, the American and his wife were found dead in their car, an obvious suicide pact. Farquar and Paul Ives were able to pack and walk away. There was nothing to sour the sweet taste of success until Paul Ives hanged himself in New York. He chose his bathroom at the Hotel Plaza, and Farquar was on his own again. He was ordered back to London immediately.

Sick with an old sickness, his mind racing backwards in self-disgust, he took a plane. Somewhere over Scotland, he shaved and was ready to go straight to Commander Scaith's home in Putney. He arrived at 8.00 A.M. Polly, the Commander's maid, greeted him and led him to a bedroom on the ground floor.

"He sleeps down here now," she whispered. "Supposed to save me the trouble of the stairs, up and down, up and down, but really it's his leg."

"Playing him up?" Farquar sympathised.

She put a finger to her lips, knocked and pushed open a door. Commander Scaith sat in an armchair in front of his breakfast tray. Farquar hesitated in the doorway. Scaith swivelled his head round sharply, an alerted mole glaring at Farquar.

"Come in, come in!" he barked. "Don't just stand there in the damned draft. Buzz off, Polly!"

Polly stood her ground. "Shall I fry a pair of eggs for Mr. Farquar?"

"Certainly not! Get his own eggs later!"

"Thank you, no, Polly. They feed you from one end of the Atlantic to the other."

"Well, you look peaky to me."

"Get out, Polly!" Polly picked up an ashtray

29

and went in her own time. "Sit down, Farquar."

Farquar took the other chair and opened his briefcase.

"I have the report here."

Scaith waved it aside.

"Office, office," he said. "Just give me the unofficial stuff. Did Ives kill himself? Or was he helped?"

"He hanged himself."

Scaith grunted. "You're getting a bad reputation, Farquar. There are those who begin to doubt you."

"That could be." Farquar thought for a moment. "My last cases have been rather tidy. Nobody left over except myself. Only my word for what happened at the bitter end."

"Yes. That's it. That's what's begun to bother people about your cases. The bitterness of the ends. We are not actually at war, you know. Why did young Ives hang himself?"

"He was not entirely a happy man, sir."

"Not entirely a happy man, sir." Scaith repeated the line. It was a habit Farquar had come to loathe: as though they were a vaudeville act, Scaith repeating the worn jokes, milking the audience for laughs, and between himself and Scaith, Farquar found very little to laugh about. "An unhappy man," Scaith went on. "So that's why he hanged himself? You'll have to do better than that, my friend!"

"The man is dead, sir. Not here to defend himself."

"Why, you dear old-fashioned thing. Not here to defend himself." Suddenly he roared. "I asked you why he killed himself, you ape! Kindly talk!"

"Paul Ives was homosexual."

"I know that!"

"Found it difficult to adjust."

"Adjust to being homosexual? Come on, Farquar. You and I both know plenty of old queens walking about. Eighty years and more! They don't do themselves in. Live and enjoy it!"

"If you must know, sir, he had rather an emotional relationship, an affair—sexual, I gather —with the American we got our information from."

"That was his function!" Scaith barked.

"Ives took his life because of a mixed feeling: many guilts involved. Primarily, I imagine, the fact that he had exploited the enormous affection he had engendered in this man. Nice man."

For once, Scaith refrained from sarcasm.

"Strange," he said broodingly. "Man will use the love of a woman, quite ruthlessly, not turn a hair. But the love of a man for a man . . . David and Jonathan . . . Ives and this American . . . " He emitted a long sigh. "And that's all there was to it?"

"That's all. The curtain comes down on most of us sooner or later. And Ives built his own gallows."

Commander Scaith dismissed the matter of Paul Ives.

"So did Philip Kimberly. Read this?"

Scaith handed the *Times* to Farquar. It was neatly folded back on two columns of the obituaries. Farquar whistled.

"Kimberly dead," he said softly.

"Yes. Scarcely believable, eh?"

"Still . . . he was sixty-two."

"A ripe age to die, in your humble opinion? Think we've all had it by sixty-two?"

Farquar tried to placate: "Well . . . no, sir . . . but—"

"But my arse! Fortunately for some of us, *your* humble opinion isn't worth a fart in a blizzard!"

"I didn't mean, sir—"

"Never mind! You've done a good job. Lost a good man, yes. But done a good job . . . "

Farquar's voice was suddenly edged: "I thank you, sir. On my behalf and on behalf of the— good man."

Scaith was not listening. His eyes had again gone to the obituary. His voice was sombre.

"Poor old Kimberly. Never met him, did you?"

"I never got the chance."

"Never got the chance." Again the reiteration; again, for Farquar, the sense of being part of a bad vaudeville act playing to an empty house, all echo and no applause. "Well," Scaith went on, "you're the loser. Kimberly. Name will always be magic. A giant of our time. They wanted him to stay on in the F.O. in '35. Everyone was after him. Could have had anything! Came to M.I.6 in '38. Saw the war coming. Kimberly: sub-Director Counter-Intelligence. Can't you just *taste* that? Then to Buckmaster in S.O.E.: boss of all guerrilla and sabotage units in occupied Europe. And when the Americans came in . . . invaluable to them So they thought. Three trips to Washington, chatting up their O.S.S. But he wasn't just a talker Brave as a lion, Philip."

Scaith sunk into a brooding silence, eyes staring at a point that did not exist. Farquar remained silent, observing the re-living of those days on the face of the old man. . . .

Scaith sighed deeply. "Made many drops into Europe Could smooth anyone down." Scaith grinned maliciously. "Especially our *friends!* Success from A to Z. Ran breathtaking risks. Even the buggering Nazis admired him. Put five million marks on his head! And, after the war— in on everything Kept popping off to Arlington to liaise with the C.I.A. And can't you just taste *that! Nothing* kept from him." Scaith chuckled with deep pleasure. "And all the while, he's arsehole buddies with good old Uncle Joe!"

"He was a traitor," Farquar said stiffly.

"Traitor?" Scaith exploded. "To whom! Member of the Party all his adult life. Got at him while he was still at Oxford. *He* was no turncoat. *We* were the bloody fools!"

"It sounds as though you admire him—sir."

"Admire him? Brilliant! Done in by the *bunglers* he was forced to work through! Tried many times to make contact with him when he started getting bored over there. Not much to keep the mind of a Kimberly fascinated in Moscow. Took to the bottle. Not all that keen on women. Except, perhaps, his lovely wife, the lovely Annabelle. And now—finished. After a life of service —did him in. Swine, eh?"

"You think they chopped him?"

"Think? 'Course they chopped him! Usefulness at an end. Becoming a bloody nuisance. Cirrhosis of the liver. Aggravated. Hah! Aggravated by a bloody *bullet* in the liver!" Scaith blinked like a lizard, looked up at Farquar. "And you never met him," he said softly. He sounded genuinely sorry for Farquar.

"I was very small fry then, sir. Just down from Cambridge. One of the swarm sent after Lady Kimberly to Lausanne, when Sir Philip surfaced in Moscow. Matter of fact, I always felt we pushed her too hard. She was hedged, poor woman. *No* way of making contact with her husband. *No* chance of his reaching her. And she wasn't really involved. Only as a wife, a mother."

"Yes . . . yes. Was only one way out for Annabelle." Scaith decapitated his cigarette viciously. "And she took it. Out of a high window. Didn't do much good for the Englishman's image."

"We looked nasty," Farquar agreed mildly. "I was in Lausanne when she killed herself. Her parents flew over to collect the little girl, poor kid."

Scaith cocked an eyebrow. "Yes. Poor kid. Never lost your interest in poor little Penelope."

"I tried to keep in touch as she grew up."

"Then it's no coincidence you've been sleeping with her for sixteen months!" Scaith managed to meld salacious appreciation with puritanical disapproval in the look he flung at Farquar.

"*Twelve* months." Farquar corrected him. "And nothing to do with coincidence. She fell in with a bad set when she came back from Grenoble University. She had a rather sordid, unhappy love affair. Didn't like it. And I was there."

"So you took advantage."

"Yes, sir."

Scaith scratched the unshaven stubble on his chin.

"Well, the Kimberly file is closed now. So you can screw her with a clear conscience."

Farquar stood up. "You will want me at the office?"

"Yes. Five o'clock. Get some rest. Have a nap."

Farquar was dismissed.

Farquar found he was still holding Scaith's copy of the *Times* as he threw his suitcase into a taxi. He glanced at it again, fascinated to find the writer's attitude resembled Scaith's: lauding Kimberly, his intellect, his capacity on the wilder shores of diplomacy and, especially, his courage. He thought of Penelope and of her own special kind of courage which her mother had not had. It must come from Kimberly.

What did she still remember of her father? he wondered. What did she remember of himself?

He had been away four months. He had seen to it that postcards reached her from various European cities and from Tokyo, places he might have visited while working with the Narcotics Division of the United Nations, which she believed to be his job. He had not wanted to break with her but felt he had no right to tether any girl. He had taken the chance of leaving it to her, to slide back to pre-Farquar days or to move on. But did this obituary change things? Would Penny now need a temporary shoulder to lean on?

As soon as he got into his own flat, he telephoned her. She was slow to answer. When she did, her "hello" was remote, uncertain.

"Penny? It's Farq."

"Oh, Farq!" she gasped. "I wasn't going to answer. They've been on to me since midnight. The newspapers. You've seen the news?"

"Yes. I just arrived. Picked up a paper."

"How did they find me, Farq? For almost ten years I've been Penny Black. Not Kimberly. Ten years!"

Farquar could feel the extent of her distress.

"They're bright boys, Penny. Would you like me to come over?"

"Oh, could you, could you!"

"Don't answer the phone again. I'll be there."

In her narrow hall, they embraced tentatively.

"You smell the same," she said. "Nice. Where are you from today?"

"All over."

"Yes. I got your cards. Just cards."

Farquar smiled wanly. "Nothing killeth the ardour of the returned lover quicker than chill in the eyes when he desires only warmth."

"The helleth with you! Some lover! Only cards!"

She laughed. He was pleased that he had made her laugh with their old joke way of talking. How could she grieve? She had been a long time away from Kimberly. She would be all right.

Her phone rang. She looked anxiously at it. Farquar went round the corner of the L-shaped room and picked it up.

"Lane's garage," he said. "Sorry, wrong number."

He hung up to break the connection, then laid the receiver on the table top.

"That won't hold them for long," Penny said. She looked at her watch. "They'll come here."

"You're right." Farquar put the phone back in its bracket. "You must come to my place."

Penny looked uncertain.

"But it's so tidy. We never make love in your place." She looked around her. "The L-shaped room: L is for love."

"Who mentioned love? Make scrambled eggs, make Buck's-fizz, yes. Love, no. Get your bag."

"I must leave a spare key for my maid." She paused. "Do you think I ought to warn her about the journalists?"

"Your maid? She's capable of seeing anyone off. But they'll have cooled down by tonight."

Penny found her spare key and her bag, checked the contents, and put a camel-hair coat around her shoulders. She tucked the spare key under the mat. In the small elevator, she leaned her back against him, stretching to rub her hair on his chin. Farquar smelled it. Christ! the smell of her hair. It was all coming back to him. He should have stayed away.

They were drinking their champagne and orange juice in bed when, out of a silence, she abruptly began to talk about Kimberly.

"I always had a loyalty to him. To my father."

Farquar saw her eyes asking for argument. "I understand," he said. "It's natural. He had much glamour. I really understand."

Penny shook her head. "You couldn't. You didn't know him. He was . . . he was so terrific. As though he never had to make up his mind. It was all there. Done. Right." She sipped from her glass, remembering. "At school, I was Kimberly's kid. And that was very good. Then, in the end, when they called Dirty Spy, I just stood there while they threw mud and gravel at me. I wouldn't move. And they were frightened of me, then. *They* were frightened. Not me." Farquar topped up her glass. This is what he had been hoping for: that she would spill, let go emotionally, and then forget.

"I didn't want to change my name to Black,"

38

she said. "But what could I do? The good old
grandparents took me for a holiday to the Lake
District It rained and rained. We went out walking with umbrellas and boots and then we moved
to London to a new flat and a new school but it
was all lies. . . .

"You see, I kept on thinking he would come
back . . . great glory and all that. It was an ad-
venture story: he never was a Russian Spy, only
Ours. I saw it all: going to Buck House with him
. . . the Queen and Kimberly's kid. . . . Of course,
time went by. I wrote to him. Still do—did. But
never a line came back. I suppose he was a-
shamed Mummy killing herself . . . all that."

"Poor blighter."

Farquar moved, settling her head more comfortably on his chest, where it had dropped.

"I thought I might hear when I was grown up.
Twenty-one got my mother's bit of money, my
own flat bought the cottage. I wrote about the
cottage because it was really a bit of luck. We
found it, he and I, years ago. We were staying
with friends and walking off a Sunday lunch. It
was so pretty It became a thing with us. We were
going to buy it when we were old. He was always
full of gin when we made plans like that, but I
didn't mind. It was going to be great when we
were old."

"Poor Penny!"

His arms retightened their hold. She felt his
deep sigh penetrating both of them.

"I'll change my name back to Kimberly," she

said. "P. Kimberly, spinster. I'm sick of lies. Nothing for me any more that's not straight out and what it seems to be. Like you, Farq. That's why I like you."

"Me! Dull as a Dover sole," he said, shrivelling within.

"You may be dull." She tried to laugh. "But you're not dull for me."

The laugh broke and turned into a flood of tears.

He comforted her.

Two

Farquar arrived at Scaith's office shortly before five. He knocked and was bidden to come in. The room had been redecorated since his last visit. He scanned the refurbished corners, looking for something to betray the past, but there was nothing evocative: concealed light where there had been a hideously ugly green glass fixture overhead.

"Like it?" Scaith asked.

Farquar nodded, managed a smile.

"All new. I didn't know."

For Farquar, it was a desecrated shrine: even the old electric kettle had gone. No more would there be the delicate aroma of China tea as it infused, while well-bred voices spoke of unspeakable things.

Commander Scaith swivelled in his new chrome-and-leather chair. He played down his disappointment.

"Bit of paint, that's all. Come in, Farquar."

Farguar was already in but took a token step forward. "A clean sweep," Scaith concluded.

"Better than a new broom," Farquar returned the cliché.

"And your friends from America: they dig it. Helps my image!"

Now he looked sly, a Jesuit fox tempting Farquar to voice his disapproval openly.

"It looks functional," Farquar conceded.

"Come, now, why so grudging in your praise?"

"Grudge yes. Praise, no."

"H. Farquar, Esquire!" Scaith laughed. "Wish I could bring you up to date as easily as I did my office. You're a fuddy-dud. Bet you're still heterosexual!"

"Boys will be boys!"

Farquar stroked his five o'clock shadow while Scaith stroked a panel, larded with buttons, by his elbow. He chose one, pressed it. The filing cabinets folded away from the opposite wall to reveal a small refrigerator and a well-stocked bar. Scaith limped across the room and leaned against the cabinet.

"All that tea I used to drink! Nobody warned me. Doing me a power of harm." His asthma racked him. "M'father's still alive," he wheezed. "Drinks whisky. Be a good fellow: get out the ice." He gestured impatiently at the refrigerator. "Glasses." Another short-tempered gesture as he plodded back to his desk, hugging a bottle of whisky to his chest. Farquar offered the ice bucket. Scaith poured his drink carefully, a well-measured three fingers. "Instant good!" he wheezed. "To my asthma. Help yourself."

Farquar found soda and mixed his drink. He raised his glass.

"Very nice. Nice improvement, sir."

Scaith glared at Farquar. *"Merde!"* he barked. "Sit down!" Scaith balanced a pair of spectacles across his nose and stared over them at Farquar. "I've read your report." He tapped the folder on his desk. "Tallies with information I've been buying. Very pricey, these days, buying information."

"Not as pricey as mine, sir." Farquar held up three fingers. "Three lives. Phut! Gone. Paul Ives swinging on his leather belt. The others . . . "

Farquar swallowed bile down with his whisky and his soda and his ice.

"Nothing for nothing." Scaith appeared smugly satisfied, his books balanced.

For a while, they discussed the new strike-plans of the American War College, which would now go to their own War Office where new British counter-plans would be devised to frustrate the American plans and which, in turn, would eventually fall into the hands of the American War College who would et cetera, et cetera, et cetera and Scaith snorted his contempt for both self-perpetuating groups, their lips pressed firmly to the public-pap, and decided the best thing would be to sell the whole bloody Island to the buggering Arabs, take their money and run, and let *them* take the final blasted loss and serve them damn well right and wasn't Farquar due for time off?

Farquar nodded. "Yes. I am due for leave."

"Then take it. Make your arrangements. Let the office know where you are, per usual. Fly somewhere, I suppose?"

"Probably."

"Reminds me." Scaith leafed through papers on his desk. "You missed the fun at the airport this morning. You were well through by then. Russian diplomat." He checked his memo pad. "Of sorts. Commercial attaché wallah. Asked political asylum as he was coming through Immigration. Arrived on Aeroflot from Moscow."

"Any trouble?"

"No. He'd managed to plant a note in English in his passport: *I ask political asylum. The men with me are armed guards. No bloodshed, please.*" Scaith snorted. "No bloodshed! Probably thinking of his own. Well, our feller, cool as a cucumber . . ." Scaith adopted the official tone: "*Just a moment, sir.*" Handed the passport and note to his mate, stepped between this Kuzminsky and his guards, probably K.G.B. Fortunately there were plenty of Special Branch about: Lord Snowdon had just taken off, and they were coming back through Foreign Immigration, not wanting to clutter up the British public like yourself on their way home."

"What did the defector do?"

"Leapt like a stag behind the desk, fell flat on his face, buried his head. Trained, I suppose.

War. There was a bit of argy-bargy, but the other two were held at bay till someone started shouting from the Russian embassy in Kensington Palace Gardens—the Lucky Number 13. Home Office will have the usual problem: is the fellow genuine or not?"

"Seems a clumsy way to plant a defector, if he's not genuine."

"Never know. The very clumsiness could be the ploy. Anyway, Home Office rang through in case we wanted to send an observer. Might be something in it for our backyard. You'd better drop in on him. The usual quarters in Whitehall until he's shipped up to Scotland for the probe."

Farquar stood up.

"If there's nothing else, I'll go now."

"Yes. Call back, let me know what you think of him. And your holiday plans."

Farquar walked past New Scotland Yard to Whitehall, his mind making bookings for the holiday.

Why fly, he thought. *Why not chunter through the night in sleeping cars?* Was there still in existence a miracle called the Flying Scotsman? That was what he'd do. He'd persuade Penelope to cut out and go with him to Scotland, putting the car on the train. Breakfast on porridge in Stirling, and motor through purple mountains to the western coast.

He strode out, already there, Penelope in proper gear keeping well up with him, and somewhere in the back of his mind the unholy cry of bagpipes. He wore a faint smile.

Fifteen minutes later, he was on the phone to Scaith.

"Kuzminsky. This morning's defector. He's changed his devious Russian mind."

"What do you mean?"

"Gone. Milroy at Special Branch tells me he was pleasant as could be in the car. Knew London. Said he'd served here before. But he pulled back."

"Kindly make yourself clear. What did he actually do?"

"Milroy took him to his own office where he hung up his own coat and left Kuzminsky with a cigarette and the *Times* while he went to arrange accommodation. In fact, he had to pop into the gents to wash his hands."

"Weak bladder."

"Possibly, sir. When Milroy got back, Kuzminsky had gone. Left by the front door, the way he'd come. It appears he may have knocked off Milroy's coat. It's missing. Milroy is charged about the coat. Apparently newish and two tickets for the F.A. Cup in a pocket."

"How does Milroy afford tickets for the F.A. Cup, I'd very much like to know! Some people . . ." The complaint tailed off. "He'll be able to sell that coat, camel-hair or some such fancy cloth the Special Branch boys swan about in. And the tickets. He'll get a good price for the tickets if he knows what he's about. Ready cash. That's the trouble, moving around with money. Check with Milroy: perhaps he knows where the seats were located. Might get a lead from that. But tell Milroy—you know what he's like—don't let him thrash around about his bloody coat. We don't want the Russian ambassador complaining we've lost their bird without even clipping his wings. Have Milroy behave *exactly* as though we still have him: breakfast tray and all that. It's important. D'you think we can count on Milroy to carry through convincingly?"

"Milroy's been Special Branch for many years, sir," Farquar said mildly.

"That's what I mean," Scaith barked, and hung up abruptly.

Farquar took a taxi home, past Penny's flat, but there were no lights in it. At home, he found a note scrawled on a last week's page torn from a small diary:

> *Press hounds baying at door when I got back but saw them from the lift and got away. Going to the cottage. Will phone, Loveth . . . loveth . . . P.*

He sighed deeply but, for Penny's sake, was glad that she had gone. There was no telephone in the cottage, nothing listed, not easy to track. He was pleased she had felt it necessary to let him know. He turned the slip of paper over. Her diary had not been very full during his absence in America. He read under Wednesday: "Hair" and

on Friday she had scribbled: "Cinema—Jim."
Jim? Who the hell was Jim? Without even the
grace to call himself James! But on Saturday, she
was alone again, the name Susan Peters penciled
in with an exclamation mark. Farquar knew
Susan always used Penny's address when she
wanted to spend the night with her boyfriend,
in case her mother telephoned. Nothing had
changed.

He poured himself a whisky, slid a cassette
into his music box, and let Brahms and travel
fatigue creep over him.

The instant Scaith cut short his conversation
with Farquar, he felt a stab of regret amounting
almost to fear Fear of what? What had he forgotten? What brisk order had he neglected to
give, not barked at Farquar? He laid his hand on
the telephone, as though by touch to restore the
broken contact He picked up the receiver. His
secretary answered.

"Nothing, nothing!" he snapped, and cradled
it again.

In self-defence, he poured another whisky.
Yet, what real concern of his was this morning's
defector? None. He downed his drink and prepared to leave the office. He pressed a bell and
received his hat and coat in silence. He gestured
that the whisky bottle be restored to its accustomed corner of the bar and the bar itself closed
up. He watched while this was done, grunted a
form of thanks, and found his stick.

In his car, he hesitated a moment and, on a sudden impulse, asked the driver to take him down the road to the Foreign Office. Even the sight of the building, he felt sure, would forge the link and remind him of what he had unaccountably forgotten to tell Farquar. But it did not. He ordered his driver to stop.

In Milroy's office, he learned that Farquar had left for home immediately after his call to Scaith. Milroy was being peevish, strutting up and down, ignoring the common courtesy of offering the lame old man a chair. He continued meticulously describing his missing coat to a Detective-Sergeant.

"Just a minute!"

Scaith rapped the desk with his cane. Milroy stopped pacing. He looked pained.

"Sir?"

"I instructed Farquar, not ten minutes past, no search was to be made for your coat."

Milroy glared.

"So you did, sir. I am now instructing the Sergeant here to stop any enquiries that may have been put under way. Though I doubt very much if anything has yet been done. It has to be murder these days before there is any hope of action, and then the fellow only gets five years because his father happened to leave home when the criminal was seven years old. And why I should lose an excellent overcoat and two F.A. Cup tickets to please your department, I would be delighted to know." He paused for breath. "Delighted, sir!"

Scaith smiled. It had suddenly come back to him: the forgotten order.

"Has this room been printed?" he asked gently.

"Printed?" Milroy was confused. "Printed?"

"Yes. Fingerprinted." Scaith's tone of laboured patience matched his small pitying smile. "I know the Foreign Office is above that sort of thing, but I want this room printed. Our missing friend may be someone we know. You told Farquar that he had served in London before. He can have been in and out of the country many times. In and out. In and out like he was in and out of your room today. In and gone again. Get this room printed tonight. By that, I mean immediately!"

Milroy was beginning to show interest.

"You think the man may be known? Wanted?"

Scaith eyed him slyly.

"Perhaps not known, Milroy, but wanted surely. I mean, he may be able to tell us where he flogged your coat, eh?" He turned to the Detective-Sergeant. "Get a print team round right away." He pointed with his cane at a mahogany chair with velvet cushions. "I presume you sat him there?" Milroy nodded dumbly. "And how long were you in the lavatory?"

"I was—"

"Doesn't matter, doesn't matter. Unforgiveable of me to ask. Curious, that's all. You may use the telephone now, Sergeant. Now."

Scaith paused at the door long enough to watch the Sergeant pick up the telephone. Milroy pulled himself together sufficiently to offer to see him out.

They waited in silence for the lift. Milroy pulled back the folding door and stood aside for a passenger to step out. The three men recognised each other. Milroy was impressed. He fluttered a little.

"Sir James!" Suddenly, Milroy was on his best behaviour. "I take it you are on your way to visit me?"

"Just dropping by." Sir James Chorley turned a beaming smile on Scaith. "Slumming, Commander?"

Chorley, always ebullient, had an air of being on a permanent holiday and enjoying it. He was Scaith's second in command, and they disliked each other in a most civilised manner: cat and dog, each purring, waiting for the other to bark.

"Just dropping by, same as you," Scaith said. "And, as I've already dropped, we won't trouble Milroy any further, shall we?"

He took James Chorley's arm, leaning on it purposefully and led him back into the lift. Scaith insisted on taking Chorley with him to his club. Chorley appeared to enjoy the ride, bouncing a little on the seat.

"Well sprung."

"Tchs!" Scaith sneered. "So you wanted to offer your sympathy for the loss of Milroy's coat."

"Simply curious, old boy. Like you." Alone, they dropped the Sirs and Commanders, indulging in plain speech. "Today's doubtful defector didn't come here for his health, I take it."

"Nor for the good Queen's blessing, or he'd be shunting off to Scotland in a comfortable sleeping car tonight instead of dropping out. Why? Why did he go on the run?"

"Why, indeed?" Chorley sighed. "Occam's Razor: let us discard all the least likely reasons and arrive at the most obvious which, as you know, my dear Scaith, is always the true one: He was appalled by the sudden thought of the London price of first-grade caviar as compared to Moscow."

Scaith glared: "And perhaps *you* will be appalled if I kick you out of this moving car onto your first-grade fat arse!"

Chorley nodded knowingly: "Ah! Then you know something about him. Something you're keeping to yourself?"

"Nothing. Milroy asked me over and I went."

"Indeed? Milroy asked you over?"

"Even a man of Milroy's mean intelligence understood there was a subtle difference in this defector cutting out. He wanted advice."

"Which you bestowed."

"Oh, indeed bestowed. With a kick in the rear end! Bloody Cup Final tickets all he cares about. And a length of vicuña. Private means. That's what it amounts to. Camel-hair. Rabbit-wool socks next!"

At the club, Chorley refused a drink. "Not thirsty, thanks."

"Don't need a thirst for whisky."

"I take whisky only when I'm feeling cold."

"Bugger you," Scaith said.

"Thank you," Chorley said.

Scaith ordered his own and Chorley, inviting himself, thought he might take a little wine with dinner.

"I'm took for dinner," Scaith lied.

"Too bad. I rather thought of fish round the corner at Wiltons'. I know you'd like that." Chorley eyed him brightly, smiling maliciously, knowing it was too late for Scaith to back out of his lie "Lashings of smoked salmon. Followed by turbot. And the Montrachet from Wiltons' special bin!" He squeezed his soft pink hands together "Num, num!"

"Damned expensive!"

"I have private means. Just like Milroy."

Scaith swallowed hard and Chorley, watching his face felt warm all over.

"Feel like lamb tonight," Scaith growled.

Chorley knew he would get nothing out of Scaith He bounced to his feet.

"Then *au revoir*." He sniffed the air. "Lamb. That's what you're going to get. But dressed as mutton."

Chorley left Scaith's club, took a few steps in the direction of Whitehall, but he knew the Foreign Office would be bolted, and Milroy already on his way to Basingstoke where he lived with a surprisingly lavish blonde from Lithuania in what could only be described as sin and splendour.

Chorley turned down a side street and into a yard and kept walking.

Scaith, at his club, finished his second whisky and went in to dine alone. He sniffed at the lamb and silently cursed Chorley.

Later he played a dull rubber of bridge which he and his partner won. They took their winnings and ordered the requisite round of drinks. The talk turned to the death of Philip Kimberly. Everyone knew he had been a great friend of Scaith but he offered no comment beyond the odd grunt which could be taken for agreement or dissent. Old Scaith was turning out to be bad company tonight and was soon left alone. Although it was against the rules, he insisted the club servant take a drink with him. The man swallowed it standing up and then saw Scaith to the door.

Scaith declined a taxi and stomped off alone towards the bus stop. He pushed belligerently in front of customers leaving a cinema. His limp and stick stood him in good stead. No one put him in his place.

Scaith preferred to dismiss his driver before dinner and anonymously find his own way home. According to his thirst and the time of night, he sometimes dropped in on friends, but tonight the conversation in the club stayed with him. Kimberly's death had stricken him. He was melancholy and was overcome by a sudden desolation.

It was the end of an epoch. There was little left.

He left the bus near Putney and took a short cut to the river front. It was his nightly habit to amble up the towpath towards his house. He had done it for twenty years, sometimes stopping for yet another drink another cloud in his darkening mind before the last one at home taken from the bottle neck before he fumbled his way to bed. But tonight the pubs were already shut and there was no one on the footpath but himself.

Scaith s leg was hurting him abominably. Sometimes he thought the day had come to have it off. He fancied himself a peg-leg like a famous predecessor in the Service. But when he studied it each morning, the leg looked sound and matched the other.

Wine was his downfall. Yet, with masochistic precision he always drank claret with his mid-day meal The pain, creeping on him as the sun went down, offered him a daily truce which he refused If a man gave up his wine, what was there left to him in the bitter end?

He brooded over the sleeping river, still thinking of the bitterness of ends. That was what Farquar had said: the bitterness of ends. Young Paul Ives Scaith had known his father Young Paul Swinging on a strap, face swollen, tongue black eyes staring at what he could no longer live with, seeing everything in those last moments seeing it for trash. Splendid limbs dangling. Well-shod feet not quite touching the tiled floor. The bitter end, meticulously measured and planned.

It was all there in Farquar's report. And where was Harold Farquar tonight? Packing his bag to go on holiday. In bed, more than likely, with Penelope Kimberly Black. Shafting Kimberly's kid. A fat lot either of them cared that Philip Kimberly was dead. The girl must be beautiful. But it was not the girl he saw like a negative of a photo developing in the moon-painted river. It was her mother's face that swam up from the mud towards him. He had been in love with Kimberly's wife. In love? He must have loved her to do as he had done. He had gone so far as to tell her he loved her. The only time in his life. He remembered going to her flat when Kimberly defected, when it was certain he would not return, news definitely confirmed that he was already in Moscow.

Annabelle Kimberly had opened the door herself. Even then, at that time, she had looked superb.

Scaith fumbled in his pocket for cigarettes, recalling details long ago denied.

She had turned him down flat—told him not to be an ass—pushed him out of the door. She could have had him, married him. But no. She shut the door.

It was then he had surrounded her, tied an army of hirelings to her. He was not going to let her follow Kimberly. She would thank him later. He left her no way. What Farquar had said: No way for her to reach Phil Kimberly. No way out —but she found one. She killed herself. Broken in every bone, sludge held together by her clothes, blood scarcely seeping through.

Scaith stood brooding, washing his memory in the river.

He tried his leg tentatively, and cursed audibly. Two people were coming towards him, walking arm in arm, whispering. They scarcely noticed him. Lovers! Always lovers! Farquar and Kimberly's girl. Kimberly and many forgotten women. Kimberly and Annabelle.

He took a few steps further up the path to a wall more comfortable to lean upon. He stared at a group of boats anchored together in a cluster like sleeping ducks just off the mud. The tide began to turn. He stood listening to the excited ripple and the sound of creaking boards, small boats waking and straining to get afloat, swinging round and pointing against the stream, towards the rumoured freedom of the sea.

Still staring over the silvered mud and waking water, Scaith dropped his match box. He cursed and poked angrily at it with his stick before making the effort to bend down.

A man suddenly stepped forward out of the shadows, bent to retrieve the box of matches, struck one and held it expertly cupped in his hand to Scaith.

Scaith concealed his surprise, eyed the man over the sheltered flame, seeing an unusual face, one he had never seen before. He bent to the flame and drew on his cigarette. The man flicked the still-burning match over the wall, a small comet, to die in the river. The precision of his gestures and his sudden appearance—breaking into his private mourning, his personal griefs—irritated Scaith.

"Thank you," he said.

He held his hand out for the match box. He received it and put it in his pocket, turning away, dismissing the stranger. But the man stood there obstinately.

"My name," he said, "is Sergei Kuzminsky." Remarkably talented as a mimic all his life, Philip Kimberly had spent innumerable hours teaching Boris Medvedev to speak English It had become a party piece to copy the Russian's careful phrasing and too-meticulous pronunciation. Kimberly used it now with every confidence. No one could have detected his own tongue. "I am the Russian commercial attaché who did defect this morning."

"Are you, indeed?"

"You are Commander Scaith?"

"More people know Tom Fool than Tom Fool knows!"

"Excuse me?"

"Matter . . . doesn't matter." Scaith impatiently threw away the cigarette he had just lit. "What do you want?"

"I come from Philip Kimberly."

"Do you? Well, my friend, you come too late. Kimberly is dead."

Kimberly bent his head, fearing that even in the darkness something of his excitement might show. News of his death had been accepted. As far as the British were concerned, he was a free man, his file closed.

"I was with him," he said. "I was with him for ten years. I was his friend."

"With a gun in his back!"

"My gun was not loaded."

"Ah! A friendly gunman!"

"Philip Kimberly told me to come to you. I am to sell documents he removed from our paymaster in 1964 before he escaped to Russia via—"

"I know the way he went: dressed as a clergyman on a day-trip to Ostend. He left us standing!"

"One-half payment for the daughter, now Kimberly is dead, one half for me."

"So he had the portfolio all the time!" Scaith leaned forward, chin jutting, eyes X-raying the darkness. "You are telling me the truth?"

"It is what Kimberly told me just before he died. He told me where I find you. I watch you go into your club. I watch you come out. I come here on same public transport. I can even take you to your home."

"Any petty snooper can do this."

"I can show you I knew him like brother. Ask for what proof you want."

"The documents will do."

"The exchange of money and of items for sale can be made in Switzerland. I will need

British passport, safe conduct, and proof money is there before you examine documents."

"How much do you want?"

"One half a million pounds."

Scaith's laugh like a bark, stabbed the night.

"Half a million! You know you are talking nonsense! And what have you done with Milroy's fine vicuña coat, you scoundrel!"

"Why you say nonsense? You have wasted more that two million pounds in last ten years to locate these documents."

"You appear to know a great deal."

"Everything Philip Kimberly knew, I know."

He reeled off a list of intriguing, little-known details of Scaith's life.

"Your price is still absurd!"

"If you cannot agree my price, the property will go on sale. Four—perhaps more—major powers will be interested. All are involved. They have trusted agents who have been in Russian pay many years. I have their names. I have proof."

"And Philip Kimberly suggested I would pay that price?"

"It is *my* price."

Scaith's face grew ugly. He had driven hard bargains before, enjoyed the marketing, but this man displeased him: the flat, monotonous voice, demanding picking a dead man's bones. Kimberly had never sold those papers, but this bastard! . . . Scaith wished him on the rack. He wanted to tear his knowledge from him, raise his stick now and strike him down. Time was . . . but now he was old, crippled, ready for the box.

He controlled a mouthful of obscenities, remembering the constable on duty near his house, a watchdog to see him safely home. It it were Grierson, and he could signal him, they would have a chance to lay hands on this over-confident "friend" of Philip Kimberly. He nearly spat, swallowed and poked his head aggressively forward again.

"At the Foreign Office? Why did you not immediately ask for me? Bargain with me in comfort?"

Kimberly sighed.

"I would perhaps have been killed in comfort before I was allowed to speak alone with you. Killed by someone named on the files I have for sale. Is very much possible."

"Yes . . . " It was a long drawn out yes, but Scaith was forced to agree. "Possible . . . " His voice again became brisk. "I will have a special line opened for you to my house for the next seventy-two hours. It will be the Putney area number: 788 . . . and followed by four zeros."

"Most useful. I will not forget."

"You have to provide something more than promises." Scaith buttoned his coat. "Something concrete before I can even approach the Treasury: solid evidence that this obscure portfolio exists."

"This is possible."

Scaith had his mind on Grierson. He turned, leaning on his stick, and began to walk slowly towards his house. Kimberly followed him warily.

"I presume you are furnished with my address."

"I know where you live."

Scaith walked on, striking at any empty cigarette packet lying in his path.

"Litter, litter everywhere," he grumbled. "Used to be a clean country. Even during the war. In Kimberly's day. Walked this way with him many times."

He was four paces from the left turn towards his house.

"Philip Kimberly has spoken to me of this river path, of your habits."

"Now, why should he have done that, I wonder?" Without turning, Scaith pointed the way with his stick. "Up here. You will reach me here."

Still at his side, Kimberly trod as carefully as a cat in enemy territory. As they turned the corner, he saw the uniformed policeman.

Kimberly was already running before Scaith's whistle screamed alarm.

Two dogs barked. A window shot up.

"That way." Kimberly called up to the gaping window sash. "He made for the boats!"

Kimberly turned left after the pub, but not before Grierson, who had been standing at his watch outside the Commander's house, saw him take off into the dark alley.

The policeman sprinted, turning left like Kimberly, but before the public house, knowing he would be bound to cut him off, unless the fellow he was after climbed the wall. So Grierson fell, tripped and stunned by Philip Kimberly, more cunning and so much longer in the game than he.

Kimberly climbed the wall and heard the dull plop of a revolver with a silencer. The impact, high in his left shoulder, sent him sprawling into the deeper darkness behind the wall.

He cursed himself as he began to run. Of course, the Soviet Embassy would have been informed how he had fled the Foreign Office. Someone there must be sufficiently in Kremlin confidence to know that a Kimberly, however much transformed, might make his way to a Commander Scaith, and a professional assassin, probably K.G.B., would be waiting there for him. Possibly the toffee-nosed Milroy himself was supplementing his income with Russian pay. He would not be the spy—Earthworm himself—but perhaps conscripted by Earthworm. Certainly, there were at least two Soviet agents within the bowler-hatted fraternity at the F.O., reporting daily goings-on.

But luck was with him: the man with the gun was too close to the constable for his own health. He quickly joined a group of people leaning over the embankment wall, watching the wild-goose chase Kimberly had set in motion amongst the boats, and from there he went quietly home.

The landlord of the pub turned on all his lights and opened his backdoor to check. He found

Grierson and dialled 999. An unconscious constable was an emergency.

In the lavatory at Putney underground, Kimberly washed and wrapped an evening paper round his arm, helping to staunch the flow of blood from the shoulder wound. He boarded the train going west and found a corner seat. He let himself be carried twice round the circuit while he recovered from shock. At Leicester Square Station he left the train and began to wander Soho streets trying to think of a safe place to look after the wound and spend the night.

Two prostitutes made overtures which he ignored, but a third, walking with a dog, appealed to him. She looked at him in a pool of lamplight.

"Blood?" she asked, touching his sleeve.

Kimberly smiled: "Nothing serious. Fighting and fucking. They go in pairs."

She answered his smile: "Well, if you're through with fighting . . ."

They walked a block together, went through a scruffy door and up a winding flight of stairs. The dog led the way.

In his own house, Commander Scaith telephoned his night Duty Officer:

"Commander Scaith here. I want Sir James Chorley. I want him now. I am at home." Scaith dialled again "Electronics," he snapped. "For Commander Scaith." He opened a small desk file and pressed the button B. He ran his finger to Black, Penelope Kimberly, 6 Granchester

Place, 229-7974. He heard a crackling in his ear and then a voice.

"Commander?"

"For experts, your line gives off a lot of noise!"

"Sorry, sir."

"Never mind, never mind! 229-7974. I want that number monitored twenty-four hours a day, starting immediately, until further notice. Report personal to me. That's all."

The man on the other end of the line repeated the number and the instructions. Scaith hung up.

In spite of the urgency and the unusual stress of his command, he had to make time for half an hour before James Chorley returned the call.

"Where the hell have you been!" Scaith barked.

"Wiltons'. Lobster and other goodies . . . "

"Listen! The Kimberly portfolio. You were wrong all along. It exists. And it's up for sale!"

"You were approached?"

"By Kuzminsky. Defector who cut out on us? And that's *why* he cut out. He was with K in Moscow when he died. Says K told him where it is. Now he wants to deal."

"You have him?"

"He ran. Knocked out a copper on the towpath. Now the Met Police will be into it. Call Sir Ronald. Now. Tell him his forces must show a low profile the next few days. The Russkies mustn't know their man tried to make a deal with me. I want them to go on believing he's held in Scotland for debriefing. Pick up his passport at the F.O.—picture and description. I want your section to catch the bastard before the police fall over him!"

"My section is strung pretty thin right now. I hear Paul Ives is back with Farquar. Let me have Ives."

"Ives is not back. Ives is dead." The silence was so complete that Scaith felt the connection had been broken. "Chorley! You there?"

"Dead? Ives is dead?"

"Farquar says he became emotionally involved on the job. One way or another. Suicide in New York."

"Luck of the draw." Chorley spoke the words singly, dropping them one by one. "But I'll still need help. Let me have Farquar."

"He's due for leave tomorrow, but I'll order him to wait for your instructions."

"Thank you, sir," Chorley said, voice subdued. "And good night."

Chorley sat up until morning, thinking of Paul Ives and of the missing portfolio . . . but mostly of Paul Ives.

Three

As Chorley finally dozed from sheer exhaustion, a catnap before going to work, Penelope phoned Farquar.

"Early bird," he said.

"I came out to buy some bread and eggs and things. I'm in the phone-box near the church."

"How are you feeling?"

"All right."

"Should you stay there alone without friends?"

"You're suggesting something."

"Well, I'm due a spot of holiday. Like me to come down?"

"What would the neighbours say?"

"I'd have thought they would appreciate a man in your life."

"Sure they would. In—all the way in. Not nibbling round the edges. Always vanishing."

"I'll come in drag and bring my knitting."

"Oh, Farq!" Her tone changed. "I feel such a fool to have bolted. What had I to run from?"

"You're entitled to privacy."

"Somewhere to cry. No good crying: it was all over years ago. Yesterday was a shock, but I'm okay now."

"When can I come?"

"Whenever you like."

"If you don't get a telegram by four o'clock, start cooking dinner for two."

"Pleasure, sir."

"Okay."

"Okay."

"Blow a kiss," he said.

"I already have. Lots. 'Bye."

Immediately after she rang off, Commander Scaith got through.

"Your line's been busy."

"Yes, sir."

"Can never get to you," he complained.

"Here I am, sir."

"Come early to my office. No." He changed his mind. "Come here. Come here now."

"A quick shave and I'll be with you."

"I am not interested in your ablutions. Get here!"

Farquar hurried. Whatever Scaith wanted, he would get it over with as soon as possible and move on to the country. He threw a few things into a bag. He had decided to take his car and drive directly on from Scaith, cutting across country. Penelope would get no telegram.

After speaking to Farquar, Penelope wandered into the hamlet to buy provisions before returning home. Her back door was warped and difficult to open. It needed both hands for the job, one to pull and the other to turn the rusted key.

She put down her bag of groceries, saw the sign, and with overwhelming certainty she knew her father was alive. That sign chalked on the step had been drawn by Philip Kimberly. She knew it without room for doubt. They had both used the sign with variations throughout her childhood in the unending game: the two of them together against the world. No one but her own father could have chalked that sign on her doorstep. He was not dead. In defiance of tall headlines and long obituaries, she knew that Philip Kimberly was alive and near to her.

The sign was quite simple. He had chalked his initial P within a circle. The tail end of the P pointed the direction he had taken. A dot within the head of the P told her to be careful: people might be watching.

It was the same signal he had left for her outside her school a hundred times, when she would find him laughing round a corner, waiting to buy her a forbidden ice-cream before escorting her back home to lunch. It was the same signal. Exactly the same.

She had fallen to her knees, almost in an attitude of prayer. "Thank God, thank God," she whispered. It took all her willpower to straighten her knees, to pull herself up by the door handle. She held it for support and fumbled for the key. Why had she locked the door? Jesus Christ! he would have been inside by now, not hiding. She let herself in and collapsed trembling onto a kitchen chair.

She lit a cigarette, drew on it deeply, dizzy and filled with sudden anguish and a new despair. It could not possibly be true. It was an illusion dreamed up to help fill the emotional vacuum she had been living in since yesterday.

She stood up and put the kettle on to boil. There was no more Kimberly. The newspaper headlines, one still lying on the table from the day before, screamed hard facts at her. Kimberly was out of the game and she, too, was released from her strange bondage to him. Her playmate was gone for good. There would be no more Indian signs. She returned to the back door and flung it aggressively open. She bent to pick up her bag of groceries.

The sign was still there.

She remained crouching down. She knew that, from where she was, she could not be observed. A thick hedge, acting as windbreak, protected the back door and continued to the shed in which she parked her car. The sign instructed her to go that way: to the garage or beyond, until she found another sign giving further instructions. A fish, for instance, would mean he was at the nearest pond or stream: a plain U sign, used so frequently, meant he had strolled to the nearest pub.

Inside the house the kettle whistled, forcing her to move. Now she must be in complete control of herself. Philip Kimberly was there and, if there were no danger and having read her message "Back Soon" chalked up on her slate, he would have been sitting on the step waiting for her. But he was not, so it was up to her to behave rationally Automatically, she put a tea bag in a cup, silenced the screaming kettle, and tried to plan. There had to be people—or at least one person—watching or covering the cottage. Else, why the warning dot in the centre of the P? The idea made her feel faintly sick: an unseen watcher in the shadows. She must appear normal, go about her day as though it were the day before yesterday, before the obituaries, or any day except today.

As she put boiling water and milk and sugar in the cup, she realised her hands were trembling again She noticed her cigarette smouldering on a plate She picked it up. Holding it in one hand, teacup in the other, she went outside: it was a habit she had, carrying her morning tea out of doors if the weather was good. She paused on the doorstep, scrambling the chalk marks with her feet. She walked casually towards the shed.

There, in the open space before the shed where she could be seen from both the road and the wood behind the house, she sipped her tea and stamped out her cigarette. She put the cup down on an upturned log. She began to collect clothes pegs off the washing line stretched between an apple tree and the shed. Gathering the pegs, she moved into the shed.

In the back of the old car, Philip Kimberly had fallen asleep of sheer exhaustion, pain from his wound urging him to let go of his senses. He was completely covered by an old plaid rug Penny used for picnicking. Only one hand was visible, palm up. She leaned down and touched it gently, drawing her finger down a well-remembered scar.

"Philip?" she whispered.

The body beneath the plaid rug stiffened. The scarred hand gripped her own. She gave a little cry of fear and pain.

"Pen?"

Kimberly let go her hand but did not remove the rug from his head.

"There's no one here, Philip. I'm sure there isn't. You can come indoors."

"Can't be sure, Pen. Listen: they've changed my face. You won't recognise me. The only thing they forgot to cover was my hand. I stuck it out for you to see but then passed out. I'm wounded, Penny. Get something to clean me up. If you have anything for pain, bring it. And drive me somewhere we can talk."

"I understand," she said, although she did not understand at all. "I won't be long."

She left the shed, picked up the teacup, and went back again into the house. She prepared

swiftly, stuffing food, antiseptic, a half-filled
bottle of Scotch, and some clean cloth torn in
strips, all into a basket. She was ready to leave
when she remembered a packet of antibiotics
left over from a tooth-abscess.

She ran upstairs to find it. She peeped out of the
small eyebrow window under the thatch. The
countryside was peaceful: the wood painted
against the sky: unbelievable to think there was
anyone out there watching, possibly with a gun.
Her own twelve-bore shotgun stood in the corner
of her room. She put some cartridges in her
pocket and picked it up. Under her coat, and
helped by the basket, she could get it to the car
unseen. Local people were used to seeing her
walk out to pot a rabbit. But not the others. Who
were the others? The unknowns who frightened
her?

Before her mother's suicide, she had known
nothing of her father's true function in life. She
thought only—and boasted of it—that he was
rather high up in the Foreign Office and had a
lot of medals from the war. He travelled a great
deal. Sometimes she and her mother and a gov-
erness would go with him. Sometimes they stayed
behind. But whenever he was there, life sang for
her. Suddenly the song had ended, broken off
in mid-bar.

After that, she had read everything there was
to read about Kimberly and Burgess and Maclean and all the other American and British

double agents. To begin with, for her it had been a search for proof that the affair of Kimberly was different from the others: that he would return, head high, from this audacious mission with a pocketful of enemy secrets for the country to digest. But, as she grew older, each news item and every book published peeled away her hopes like onion skin, until only a tiny kernel of belief in Kimberly remained, fermenting in her unconscious.

When she had troubled dreams, cried out in her sleep, he still emerged heroic, saving her. That was why his hand was scarred, gashed and badly repaired after saving her from a blazing nursery Only he got in, smashed glass and fought his way out with her. Only Kimberly. The smell of smoke was always in the nightmare, stifling her till she woke choking. Asthma, the doctors said, and treated her without success.

She felt breathless now, gasping for air. She fought the condition, forcing herself to fill her lungs slowly and deeply and exhale calmly. Three times she went through the exercise. Surely this sudden death and resurrection of her father would expose the truth at last! Breathe in, breathe out. That was better.

She hid the gun under her coat, picked up the basket, locked the door and went back to the shed. The man was still there, crouched low in the back seat, completely covered by the rug. She put the basket beside the driver's seat, and slid the gun in after it.

She got into the car and drove out without speaking a further word.

At Scaith's house, Polly had set a table in the front room. Today Farquar was offered breakfast. He sat down before a plate of ham and eggs.

Scaith was already dressed in office clothes. Blue and white striped shirt, dark tie and highly polished shoes set the tone. Though he wore a cardigan, a small concession to comfort in the home, his double-breasted jacket hung waiting on the back of his chair.

Farquar sensed tension, a spiritual clearing of the decks for action. The querulous old boy of yesterday had gone. Scaith had the air of Lord Nelson ready and eager to raise the telescope to a blind eye and forge ahead.

Farquar dropped a lump of sugar in his teacup and picked up the simple Georgian spoon.

"Nice of you to see me so early, sir. I can still get on my way in good time."

Scaith offered him the toast rack. "Planning something special?"

Farquar mixed his sugar and milk and tea. "Country," he said. "Roam a little. Visit friends."

"Good." Scaith brought his hands together with a satisfactory clap and wrung them in self-approval. "Then there is nothing definite. Nothing that can't wait. Good lad."

"Actually I—"

Scaith refused to hear him. "Knew I could count on you. Something has come up."

He raised a laden fork to his mouth and gestured to Farquar's plate. "Eat," he ordered, mouth full.

"Yes, sir," Farquar sighed.

The jaundiced eyes of his two eggs mocked Farquar from his plate. Scaith pushed the salt-cellar towards him while he chewed and washed his breakfast down with tea. Finally he wiped his lips with a fine damask napkin and settled back in his chair. He told Farquar what had happened the night before, underlining the importance of the missing portfolio.

"So it boils down to this," Scaith concluded: "We must lay our hands on it. If Kuzminsky comes back to me, Treasury will have to pay up. Meanwhile, we'll not be sitting back. It's up to us to smell him out and then—squeeze." He gestured with his hands. "Squeeze! Which would give me the greatest pleasure!"

"Could it be," Farquar suggested, "a have-on by an opportunist par excellence? Taking advantage of the crucial hour? He starts his term of foreign duty the day after Philip Kimberly dies. The whole plan suggests itself. Yes, he may have known Kimberly. No reason why not. There's always been rumor among the brethren about a missing Burke's Peerage of sleeping Russian agents. The rest he invents."

"He invented nothing. He had details of my life only Kimberly could know. Only Kimberly!"

But it was too bizarre a story for Farquar to digest with breakfast.

"I still can't see it, sir. I can't believe papers of that importance, missing for ten long years, time ticking away . . . "

"Not *missing*! This portfolio has never been missing. It's been carefully hidden by a man who knew his job, a man who, when he knows his end is near, wants to put his books in order. A man of such expertise would want the ledger to tot up and balance. So he passes the information on. He does not need that protection anymore. He's had his chips and, as you and I both decided yesterday, he is his own executioner. It's his friend Kuzminsky who turns rogue, wants to cash in."

Scaith stood up and reached for his city jacket. He wanted no further argument. Yet Farquar felt bound to continue his protest.

"Something smells," he said.

Scaith stood over him in his shirt-sleeves, body bulging beneath fresh linen.

"Smells! Not as badly as it will smell if Comrade Kuzminsky sells those documents above our heads, proves to the world in general that we've been breast-feeding another Kimberly throughout these years: a top man to us and working for the Russkies all the time! Kimberly was a prototype worth copying, don't you think? Why not a Cabinet Minister? A *Prime* Minister? Have you no imagination, Farquar? Have you never considered the possibility that I *myself* could be Earthworm? Information leaking all the time.

Why *not* me, eh? There were dozens in those days flipped and signed on with the Russians. What's become of them? Those documents will tell a lot!"

"Signed during the war."

"Oh, yes! Yes, sir, indeed sir!"

"With the country almost on its knees."

Scaith snorted: "No worse than it is now! No buggering Arabs screwing us then!"

Farquar felt a rare upsurge of sudden anger.

"But then the country was bleeding to death. *Literally!*"

Scaith blew his cheeks out, face turning a delicate shade of puce. "Please! Please, Farquar! Please try not to sound more of a fool than you are! The Russkies were our husky allies. Pictures of Churchill in the press, teamed up with Roosevelt, hugging the avuncular Mr. Stalin! Everybody cut them out, stuck them up behind the clock on the chimney-piece! Oh yes! Not hard at that time to persuade some bleeding-heart, some pseudo-idealist that he was looking ahead! A visionary! If you wanted a bit of dirty work done with enthusiasm, it was all in the cause of preparing for a better world, creating a new language between men of Brotherly Love and Kiss Kiss Kiss. With a Russian accent!"

He turned away, fitting his coat, buttoning it.

"Is that all, sir?" Farquar asked quietly.

"No! That is not all, sir! We had the Germans to hate then! Or do you not recall Mr. Hitler?

Those were great days for conscripting spies. Things have gone to the dogs since then. There'll be talk of old-age pensions for them soon. Or getting their cards stamped!" He began to admire himself in the mirror. Farquar bent over his cold eggs and attacked them like an enemy. "Do you know James Chorley?" Scaith added abruptly.

Farquar smiled. "Sir James?"

"That's right. Sir James. Tried to call himself Hamish for a while but it didn't jell. So you know him?"

For some reason, Farquar was still smiling. "I don't know him well. In fact, hardly at all. From what I've heard, he appears to have great charm."

"You think so? Well, this charmer has asked specifically for you. He wants none other assigned to him in the matter of unearthing this Sergei Kuzminsky and the elusive Kimberly portfolio."

Farquar wanted desperately to save his holiday.

"Find and Hold: not exactly in my field, sir."

"I know that and you know that. But it's you that Chorley wants. Your reputation is evidently ahead of both you and me, Farquar!" He turned to the door, paused in its frame. "He will be in touch with you."

Farquar rose. "Yes, sir."

"Sit down. Ask Polly for a fresh pot of tea." Scaith ordered, still hesitating in the door. "You'll have a chance to find out just how charming Sir

79

James Chorley really is. And you're to report in detail to me. Direct."

"Yes, sir."

"And if you happen upon the Kimberly strong-box, I want these documents brought straight to me." He paused. "Unread. Understood?"

"Understood, sir."

"I will make myself responsible for summary justice. There will be no further scandal while I am in this driving seat." He touched his tie once more, felt his left lapel, searching the button-hole, missing the *Legion d'Honneur*. "Well, there you are," he said, and left.

Farquar refused Polly's efforts to mother him. Uttering thanks for his breakfast, he backed down the short path to his car. The holiday was off. He drove east instead of west. He had to send Penelope a telegram. He parked his car and carried his bag up to his flat. There would be no dinner for two in the small cottage near the woods.

Feeling melancholy, Farquar unpacked and then took a taxi to his office, waiting to hear from Sir James Chorley.

Twice during the morning the Foreign Office phoned through to Commander Scaith. They were concerned about Sergei Kuzminsky. The Russian Embassy was playing hell with them and they were running out of lies. Had the Commander any news?

"Nothing to do with me," he growled at his secretary. He grew petulant. "They had him, let the blighter go. Let *them* find him. What's it got to do with me? No! I will *not* speak to them!"

His secretary, an extremely handsome lady, kept looking at Scaith, scribbling on her pad as she spoke soothingly into her telephone:

"Yes. I do understand the urgency. I'll see he gets the message. No, I cannot say. Yes, I do. Thank you very much." She raised her eyebrows. "Naughty, naughty, Mr. Blore! Good-bye."

Scaith eyed her over his spectacles. "Flirting!" he barked. "Waste of time. The other thing . . . well, now—that's worth a bit of trouble. But flirting, no!"

He leered.

She picked up her pad and went to her own desk to type the message from the Foreign Office. All communication was preserved in black and white and later microfilmed and stored in huge vaults built to withstand a nuclear bomb, deep underground in the heart of the country.

When she had finished, she laid the memorandum on his table. He read it.

"See what I mean?" Glaring, he pointed to the note. "Since I *chose* to send *my* Mr. Farquar from *my* department to see Kuzminsky yesterday et cetera and et cetera and et cetera. *I* chose! See their devilish cunning? I did not *choose!* I was *invited!* And that is a request, is it not? And do I often refuse a simple, humble request?"

The telephone interrupted him. She answered it, repeating the name. "Sir James Chorley? I'll see if the Commander is available," but Scaith's hand was already on his own instrument. She pressed the connecting button.

"Well?" Scaith barked, and listened in silence. The Russians were demanding that Kuzminsky be returned to them at once. They claimed he must be treated not as a political, but as a common criminal who had abused his position as a commercial attaché to falsify accounts and systematically steal from the State. He had been brought to London, where most of the major juggling had taken place, to be faced with irrefutable facts. They insisted this was his only reason for defecting at the airport. They are now demanding that Her Majesty's Government hand him over to the Russian authority forthwith.

"Uppity, aren't they?" Scaith said. "Damned uppity! Which, for me, only underlines the truth of our friend's story. Does give it body, don't you think? Farquar's been briefed. Waiting to hear from you. He's all yours. Good-bye." He turned to his secretary. "Telephone the Foreign Office. Tell them, since they press me for it, my advice is to inform the Russian Ambassador that their defector was injured while trying to leave a moving train that was taking him to the country for interrogation. His condition is serious. The medical officer will allow no visitors at present. The Soviet Embassy will be kept informed."

His secretary put down her pad and pencil. "You see why I never ask for your advice?" she said.

Four

Penny drove through the open gate. "I'll give you a sort of running commentary," she said. "Reorient you. You remember the village is on the right. I'm going to take the back road round it. The church is Norman and—God, I sound like a ten-penny guide book!"

She drove on in silence for some minutes, her mind scurrying for refuge here and there. Yesterday this man had been acknowledged dead. What was he running from? He was a famous Russian . . . British . . . Russian . . . British . . . he was a famous spy. Why was he crouching in her car? He said they'd altered him. They. Who? There was a lot of explaining due to her.

Kimberly was thinking along the same lines. What would she accept as truth? He must not think of her as a twelve-year-old child. What could she be expected to believe? Truth? Well, as much as possible . . .

"That's it," Penny said finally. "Village past.

No one taking any notice of us. I think you can come up for air."

But Kimberly still made no move. She gathered speed. "There's a bit of new road here," she continued. "Only about two miles. Then I'll cut off toward the common and we can stop. It's still exactly the same: plenty of scrub and trees . . . rabbits."

When Kimberly felt her slowing down, heard her change gear, felt the car swerve and then the rough surface of the smaller road beneath the wheels, he begun to move. His body was cramped, his shoulder throbbing and his head swimming from pain and loss of blood. He made a tremendous effort, putting both hands on the back of the front seat and raising his head. The rug slipped away.

Penny saw the face in her rear-view mirror and screamed. The car swerved wildly onto the grass beside the track. She screamed again and again.

Kimberly leant forward, grabbing the steering wheel. Penelope had completely lost control of it. She clutched for the door handle. All she wanted was to get out, get away from this frightening fake and run.

"Penelope! Stop it! Stop! I told you they had changed my face!"

The car lurched to a halt, half off the road. He had his arm under her chin, holding her helpless. Their eyes met again in the mirror—the tilted Slavic eyes and her own green almonds. She stopped screaming and let out a low moan of terror.

"Penny. I warned you. Yes, it's a shock,—a nightmare. But you must believe it's me. You saw my hand."

He released his hold, raising his right hand in front of her eyes.

"Please. Let me go. Please let me go," she moaned.

Abruptly, he released her completely. "Yes. I'll leave you here. You can drive away."

He got out of the car painfully. She watched his movements closely, alert for a sudden move. He put his right hand inside his coat to touch his wounded shoulder. She raised her gun quickly, the barrels pointed straight at him through the open window of the car.

Kimberly's face creased with a twisted grin, something about it faintly recognisable. "Put the pop-gun away, Piddle-Pee," he said. "Someone has already done it for you."

He withdrew his right hand from his shoulder and held it up. The scarred hand was now covered with blood.

Penelope gasped, let the gun slip back onto the seat, covered her face with her hands. Everything was terribly wrong. He'd said his face was changed. She had visualised some scar. Not this mask. But the childhood name, his voice, the words he used—it all added up to Philip. Tears oozed through her fingers.

Kimberly went round to the other door and

reached into her basket. He prodded the contents and brought out the whisky.

"Not supposed to be the best thing for a bleeding wound. Let's risk a little." He unscrewed the bottle and took it round to her. "Nibble a bit." She shook her head, slanting another look at him. He raised the bottle to his lips. "Here I go again: drinking on an empty head."

He took a long swig. Penelope pushed her hair back from her face, knuckle-wiped her eyes, frowning deeply.

"Yes. Philip. I know it's you. It's really you. But I'm frightened."

"Yes. I know. And's it's good to be frightened. Part of the survival kit. But you need have no fear of me." He reached out and gently touched her cheek. She nodded her head, her hand closing on his own. Kimberly's smile was tinged with sadness. "Right. Now, I'm going to get back into the car. You're going to drive up there—that spot at the top of the hill where we can see everyone and no one can see us. You know the place."

"I'm relieved you do."

He got into the car. Penelope laid her hands on the steering wheel but made no move to start the engine.

"We'd better move, Pen."

"I still feel zigzag."

"May not have much time. Very smart lads after us. Very jet-propelled."

"After *us*?"

"I phoned your flat often as I could yesterday.

No answer. Knew I had to get here to warn you. Was afraid they'd already picked you up."

"Picked me up? Who? Why *me*?"

"Drive, Pen," he said gently. "I'll try to explain." His grin was bitter. "Much as is good for you to know." She switched on the engine and moved the car onto the road. "The Russians. I spoiled their plans when I cut loose yesterday."

"Why did you?"

"Because they pushed me into a plan where all I could win was a second obituary. Now, they'll try to use you to bargain with me, force me back. That's what I feared."

She glanced at him quickly. "You feared for *my* life," she said flatly.

Kimberly nodded, again with that melancholy smile.

"Paternal instincts seem to die hard. Before I left England, I removed very secret, very important files from the Russian paymaster here. Only I know where they are. Thought I might be able to use them as an insurance policy to get you and your mother brought to me." He sighed deeply. "Damned unrealistic. . . .

"But, as you can imagine, there was little time that last, frightening day before I had to go. Your mother wanted to up-sticks herself and trek with me. But it wasn't possible. And, in any case, I wouldn't let her come. Not then. I wanted her to be able to maintain her position as an innocent. Your mother . . ." He broke off and Penelope felt his effort to swallow another deep sigh.

"Amazing woman. Ardent communist. Militant. But subtle. No one knew. Only myself and two others When we first met, I was Left, of course. Oh, very much so. Enthusiastic. But undisciplined. And she taught me. Taught me how to dissemble To use the right hand instead of the left. Taught me to . . . I wanted to shine for her. I did shine Very sad."

He fell silent and the silence hung heavy between them. The car began climbing.

"We're nearly there," Penny said. He did not answer. She cast a side look at him and saw his eyes were closed. "Not far now," she encouraged quietly. "No need to talk further."

"No," he whispered. "No need . . . no need . . ."

When they were settled, the car hidden by trees and the broad downs spread at their feet, Penny showed him her half-packet of pills. He studied the box and swallowed three of them.

She got out of the car, spread the rug, and helped him peel off his coat and shirt. He lay face downward on the rug. She dressed the wound as he directed her.

"Just do as I say. Even if I swear at you. Just keep telling yourself it's not going to hurt you. Efficient field orderlies do that and they save lives. Maybe we can save a wing."

The bullet, entering high on the shoulder blade, had been deflected as it struck bone and emerged in a mess of torn flesh.

Penelope poured antiseptic into the entrance

wound and plugged it. He shifted and groaned deeply and for some time he lay motionless. She touched his neck beneath the hair, trying to sooth the nerve-ends. She felt the well-healed scars where the loose flesh had been pulled up.

"All right?" she asked. "Let's turn the body. Heave!"

He turned painfully over. She began on the exit wound, picking small splinters of bone off the torn flesh. He kept his eyes closed, sweat bursting on his upper lip and forehead. He began to speak thickly, from his throat.

"No one you can trust." He drew breath sharply between clenched teeth. "No one . . . not —anyone . . . "

She bandaged the arm in silence. She brought the whisky bottle to his lips and poured a few drops onto his clenched teeth.

"Please. Try to swallow."

She repeated the dose several times. He seemed to relax and she thought he was asleep. But when she moved, he gripped her.

"You mustn't go to your flat or your cottage again," he whispered. "If they take you, you'd be in Moscow by midnight. There would be no way out."

She saw the effort of talking was exhausting him. She soothed him and he let her go and soon he was asleep. She sat beside him, trying to re-press the terror she was starting to feel deep inside.

Later she drank a little whisky and ate a piece

of bread. She noticed he was breathing with less difficulty, and his pulse, when she felt it, was steady and surprisingly strong. She put her coat over him and walked around the hillock, keeping in the cover of the trees. A few grazing cows were the only sign of life. From the distance she heard the faint barking of a dog. She made the tour several times. She saw no one. Nothing changed. The dog barked on.

An hour passed before his eyes opened again. A few wisps of cloud flirted with the sun in the pale blue sky on which his gaze seemed fixed. She saw two tears glide out of the strangely slanted eyes.

"Well! A very lovely day," she said, dredging a few prosaic words to cheer him.

He sat up slowly, leaning on his good arm. "Yes. Lovely day. Except for the mess, eh? What a mess I've made of things! For everyone!" He spoke with sudden, hard decision. "You must get out of here. Buzz off to Scotland. Stay with the MacGregors."

"And you?"

"I have unfinished business here."

"Like dying?"

"I'm not quite ready to die yet."

"In that case, I'm going to drive you to a place where no one will find you or bother you for a few days. A pub owned by friends of mine. I can explain you're an eccentric uncle on the run from a looney-bin."

"You wouldn't be exaggerating."

Youth still on her side, she laughed spontaneously and held out her hands to help him up. But with touch, her laughter died. What had they done to him? What would they do to her? She looked at him somberly.

"What would they do with me in Moscow, as you're so important there?"

He knew what they would do with her, and he knew the K.G.B. knew that he knew.

"Lubianka Prison," he said. He wanted to frighten her, yet not too much. "But Lubianka is not too bad," he lied.

She picked up the basket, knowing that he lied, and they drove off.

Penelope left him in the car outside the Bull Hotel. She walked through the reception hall into the back of the hotel, calling for Douglas Ransom. He greeted her with pleasure.

"I'm in a bit of a spot," she explained. "Actually, it's a friend of mine. The bailiffs are after him to serve a writ, and they musn't. He'd lose his job. It's only a matter of getting his lawyers to sort it out, but he's been ill and simply had to have a few days without being pushed."

"He can stay until Friday. We're booked for Easter."

"That's fine. The bailiffs go holy until after Easter. Can you cash me a cheque?"

"I can give you twenty pounds. I'll put it on the bill. Okay?"

Penelope gave him a quick kiss on the forehead and hurried out to Kimberly.

"You're in." She gave him a brilliant smile. "Your name is Farquar. Harold Farquar. Don't forget it."

"Farquar? What a name to choose!"

"My boyfriend. So at least I won't forget. Your address is 4 Peter Street, S.W.I. Just sign in, say you're feeling awful, go upstairs, and have a nap. I'll shop for a razor and this and that, and be back by lunch."

Kimberly followed her in silence, pondering the new element flung at him. Now he was a Harold Farquar: his daughter's lover, apparently, whose name he was adopting to sign the hotel register. He shook hands with Douglas Ransom, and his wife, Pauline, appeared. She took Kimberly upstairs, clinking keys. Douglas turned to Penny, raising shaggy eyebrows.

"Bit old for you?"

"Oh, come off it, Doug. That man was bloody good to me. Actually, he paid for an abortion. Wasn't even his. For God's sake, don't let on to Pauline. She still tries to mother me."

Thus Penny built up a conspiratorial bond. Douglas walked with her to the car, held the door open for her. "What's the gun for?"

"Bailiffs."

Douglas grinned, flagged her onto the road, and went back to the hotel. Pauline Ransom was studying the register.

"Harold Farquar. I've heard Penny speak of him. Poor fellow looks worried to death."

"Bailiffs," Douglas said. "Penny says they're hounding him."

"Bugger bailiffs." Pauline put the book away. "Rot them. I can do without that lot."

Again, Douglas grinned. "Penny's carrying a gun for them."

"Gun? I'd carry a red-hot poker and I'd poke it you-know-where!"

"My, my," Douglas said mildly. "Treat them like royalty, eh?"

Pauline moved off to the kitchen, calling for him to carry in some logs.

Now that she was on her own, Penny felt the nervous reaction set in. She had overcome her first terror at Kimberly's altered appearance. The necessity for physical action had kept her on an even keel. The wounded man lying prone, needing her help, calling on her resources as a human being, kept her balanced. Controlling fear and nausea, matching herself to his stoic acceptance of unskilled hands doctoring him, she had come through well. Now, however, with Philip bandaged, resting, and temporarily safe (safe from *what*?) she had time to think.

She would have to telephone Farquar, put him off. No. Not yet. She might break down. That would help no one.

No. She must first give Philip time to explain before running for help. The possibility of a personal assault upon herself she was trying to dismiss as fiction. Here in pastoral England? It seemed like the raving of a sick man in delirium. Yet was he delirious? No, not really.

She parked the car and walked to the chemist shop, producing the empty box of antibiotics.

"I know I should get a prescription," she admitted. "But I haven't been here long enough to get on the National Health and my tooth abscess has come back." She rubbed her jaw. "Perhaps you could help me this once . . ."

She looked so genuinely tired that the chemist broke the rule and sold her a packet of the drug, along with a toothbrush and some dentifrice, soap, shaving cream, and a razor. She also purchased a large bottle of powerful antiseptic.

Penny's head was aching, a dull, pounding ache like that of an abscessed tooth, but she did not want to go back to the Ransoms yet. They would be less likely to have time to question her when the lunchtime trade was in full swing.

She went across the road to a coffee shop, ordered a pot and lit a cigarette. A pay telephone in the corner mesmerised her. It would be so comforting to speak to Farq. The waitress offered a morning newspaper. Today there were no headlines about Philip Kimberly. So quickly past, she thought dead and, so far as the world was concerned, already buried.

She ruffled through the paper. Kissinger was back, dominating the news. . . . And a policeman had been assaulted—skull cracked on a paving stone while he was chasing a burglar who appeared to have got away by boat somewhere above Putney bridge. . . . Ah, here was a bit about Kimberly: someone suggesting a memorial service.

Penny felt sick. Suppose he did die? Suppose his arm festered and he died of blood poisoning? She would be responsible. She should have got a doctor, no matter what he said. She paid her bill and asked for change to telephone. There was no reply from Farquar's flat. She got her coins back and dialled his office.

"Farquar here."

His office voice. She knew she could not tell him her story now. To begin with, it was beyond belief. There was no way.

"It's Penny," she said.

"Penny! Where are you?"

"In the country with some friends who run a pub." That much, at least, was true. "Douglas and Pauline Ransom."

"Don't think I know them."

Even speaking to him—even his office voice— cheered her.

"You don't. You're my London lover, remember? These are country friends."

Farquar laughed: "What can the London lover do for you that the country lover doesn't know how?"

"Plenty. But first I'm ringing to put you off."

"Then you haven't had my telegram doing the same to you?"

"No, Farq. But I changed my mind as soon as I went back from calling you. Suddenly it seemed so dreary at the cottage. And I have work in London early tomorrow. All day at the Dorchester. A conference. It didn't seem fair to drag you down for just one night."

Farquar had visualised that night and the cottage as she had described it: under the thatch, the two of them more alone than they had ever been before. Well, there would be other times. He had made up his mind there must be other times. Odd, though, that she had changed her mind. Still, as things had turned out for him, it was just as well.

"When will you be coming up?"

"Listen, Farq." She hesitated. "Could I sleep at your place tonight?"

"Morning coffee will be sixpence extra."

"Idiot! I know the papers have nearly let the Kimberly story die, but I thought I'd give it another day before going back."

"I'll be at the flat by six. Don't be late."

Penny felt happier. Farq was there: solid, sensible, available. She settled with the waitress and drove back to the Bull Hotel.

Penny went straight up to Kimberly's room. He had locked himself in. She knocked. He opened the door cautiously.

"I've got some things for you and more pills," she said. She put them on the bed and looked at Kimberly. He was less pale. "Do you feel well enough to shave and join me downstairs for lunch?"

"I'd better not sit round a pub."

"It might be less noticeable."

"If your friends ask, say I'm not feeling too well."

"Pauline Ransom's a bit of a fusspot—she might call for a doctor pronto! But shouldn't you have a doctor, Philip? He won't know who the hell you are."

"Don't you know he must report a gunshot wound to the police?"

"You could insist it was an accident."

Kimberly remained adamant. Penny saw it was no good arguing further. She went down to the hotel kitchen, squaring herself with the staff. She begged a tray to carry some cold snacks upstairs for Kimberly and herself, passing by the bar for beer. There she almost made her first mistake, stumbling between the names Philip and Farq. "He thinks he's getting flu," she explained. "Doesn't want to spread it round. Bit of a hypochondriac, I think."

"What man isn't," Pauline Ransom grumbled, glancing at her husband. "Douglas cries for an oxygen tent if he so much as sneezes!"

Kimberly opened the door and took the tray from her. "God!" he said. "English bangers!" He picked up a sausage in his fingers, dipped it in mustard, and began devouring it. "Between English bangers and that wash and shave, I'm back on my feet!"

He spoke with his mouth full, looking younger and far more hopeful. Penny thought she could see a trace of his own looks breaking through the mask as he sat on the bed, eating with his fingers and reaching for the pint of beer.

Kimberly knew his tactics were sound. His stock in trade had always been near genius in promoting friendly relations. He had a way of always pulling from his carpetbag just what would amuse and please. Penny had looked almost sulky when she went downstairs. An apprehensive, sulky girl would be no help to him. It was ten years since he had seen her. Vis-à-vis himself, she was a daughter twelve years old, a little girl who had loved her Dad, not some Gothic fright-figure with plastic fangs. She had been his pal. She would be his pal again. He put a slab of cheese on bread.

"Mousetrap. I have missed my mousetrap cheese." He caught her smiling. "Actually, I've missed a hell of a lot."

He talked of things in the past, things which touched her and things which made her laugh, and by the time he had finished his lunch, a new warmth had been created between them. Then he told her that he had finally reached a decision but would rather discuss it out of doors because all walls have ears and she realised he meant that seriously.

"Not in England. Certainly not in the Bull Hotel. But let's go, anyway. I want to be back in London by six."

He made a move, his back against the door, barring it.

"Why? Where are you going? You can't stay at your place."

"I'll be with a friend. And I do have my living to earn," she reminded him. "I'm a clever girl. I speak four languages fluently. I take shorthand and I type and I even plodded through a Russian course. I thought it might please you."

"Yes. You wrote to me."

"Why did you never answer?"

He evaded the question. "Come. Let's go."

She picked up the tray. He took it from her, his left arm, still slightly awkward, pressed into his side.

Douglas Ransom was mopping up the bar. He found himself feeling uneasy about Penny's friend. She had explained his trouble, but in Douglas's world a man reacted differently if a hand was held out to help him through. He might have been expected to come down, perhaps drink a little too much from sheer relief at finding himself, even temporarily, amongst people who were on his side. But this man . . . well, he just vanished like a mole into a hole. Douglas hoped he wasn't having Penny on with a sob story. Yes, he may have helped her in the past, but in Douglas's book, that's what it was all about. Being people.

"Feeling better?" he asked Kimberly.

"Yes, thanks. Going for a stroll."

He put the tray down on the bar and took Penny's arm. She felt his muscles tense, urging her to the door. Outside, he turned towards the car park.

"I thought I'd take the train," she said. "Parking in London is a bore if I'm not in my own pad. And the trains go every half hour."

"Then I'll take you to the station and fetch you when you come back."

She seemed doubtful. "But what about your arm?"

"Not too bad. I'll be able to drive. You show me the way and I'll find my own road back."

Penny could not help feeling he was anxious to be alone. Perhaps not a bad idea: he might relax and get more rest. She got into the driving seat and moved the car out onto the road.

Kimberly asked for a cigarette. She handed him the pack. He lit up and smoked nervously. Suddenly he stubbed out the cigarette and began to speak in tight, clipped tones.

"Never wanted to go, to leave England. Even the bungling asses running the country were good to me. Complete idiots. But men of heart. Which, unfortunately, is not enough." He brooded for a moment. "Can't pretend I went to Russia unprepared. Knew damned well that vast omelette hadn't been made without breaking eggs: bloodshed unequalled in history. I'd accepted that as historical necessity. But the blood just never stopped flowing. Cause drowning in it. Only effect left. Became terribly disillusioned. Watched the centres of power grow ever larger horns and fangs and claws. So I drank. And heavily. Became the amusing buffoon. But finally an embarrassment. It was soon clear: Kimberly had to go." He chuckled, bitterly amused. "And that's what put them on the horns. They knew it could only have been I who removed their files. Otherwise, a bullet behind my ear would have solved their problem. So some mastermind dreamed up this masquerade. All those months in hospital. Pruned like a bloody tree. And no one to speak a word to except Boris."

"Boris?"

"A friend."

"Friend! What sort of friend to sit by and—"

"Oh, no. A friendly friend. But impotent. Like me."

"Where is this Boris now?"

Kimberly paused, considering what might have become of Boris Medvedev. He sighed deeply.

"Ah, poor Boris. More than likely dead."

"Why?"

"Because I was flown here in his custody. He was responsible for me. I was to turn the files over to him. For this, I was to be given a new name, a new passport, a new life with a fortune in Switzerland and, finally, a comradely farewell. Well, Penny, I knew what the comradely farewell would be once I produced the files: my comradely body interred in a comradely limepit." Again, he fell into a brooding silence, and Penny, barely breathing, eyes fixed on the road ahead, waiting for him to continue. "Penny . . .

I don't think I've too long to live, in any case.
Liver is all shot. But the documents I have could
save the lives—British and others—of many
thousands in any coming war. Moscow has top
agents buried deep in England and other coun-
tries. All men in high places. Safe. Beyond sus-
picion. *They* know they are named in the files.
That's why I went on the run from London. Nowhere am I safe. If I fall into the wrong hands
here, they will quickly turn me back to the Russians as the unacceptable defector named Sergei
Kuzminsky."

"But there must be someone, someone you can
trust! Someone I could speak to for you—"

"No! No one! You speak to no one! Not even
your closest friend!" He controlled himself with
effort, spoke in a softer voice. "Penny—listen to
me. I've trusted you. I could have picked up the
documents, made my deal. But I had to warn you
to take care until I am out of the country again.
If you let me down, I will be a dead man. In the
first few hours, they were after me with a gun.
But I had to think of you. And now, if you should
blunder in trying to help me, speak in confidence
to your friend—to anyone—he would be bound
to take your information straight to the Foreign
Office, no matter how devoted he may be to you.
And I will be dead."

"Oh, no, Philip, no! I promise. I'll speak to no
one." She pulled up at the station and reached
into her handbag as they heard the train approaching. "Philip, take this money. All I need

is my fare. I'll go to my bank tomorrow. I've got about two hundred pounds saved. You can have that, too, if it will help. I'll be in touch."

Impulsively, she kissed his cheek, and ran for the train. It was comparatively empty and she flung herself into a corner seat.

Philip Kimberly watched Penelope's train start toward London. He moved into her driving seat. He adjusted the driving mirror, studying his face thoughtfully. He expected that, as a wanted man, there would soon be a description of him circulating amongst the police as well as the K.G.B. He would have to re-disguise himself but that should not be difficult.

He had a car and money and a place to sleep the night. His arm was not too much of a handicap. He was certain he would be able to drive with ease, nor had his memory failed him. He had recognised the lie of the land. In spite of the new roads, he was fully oriented. He had to go to Woburn and on toward Oxford, stopping in a market town. But first things first. He left the car and bought himself a newspaper.

He saw from the front page that the policeman who had got in his way at Putney had fallen heavily and cracked his skull. Evidently, he was something of a local hero on the football field. They ran a picture of his thin young wife, and blew up, in journalese, Kimberly's own run down the towpath that set off the wild-goose chase. One witness had described his as a "toff." Kimberly smiled: there was no mention of his meeting with Commander Scaith. The old boy must be going berserk waiting to hear from him again.

Kimberly began his drive. He would phone Scaith tomorrow morning. One more night for the old boy to stew. When it was all over, he would let him in on the secret: his old friend Phil Kimberly had risen from the dead.

Kimberly knew that Scaith could never admit the truth to anyone. It would be the ultimate loss of face. He grinned his new, tight grin, picturing Scaith, probably with a passport in hand ready for him now. Scaith waiting! What else could he do? The international situation could not be worse, nor better for Kimberly's purpose. War in the Middle East imminent, Moscow and Washington shaking hands, but with a wrestler's grip, each ready to throw the other out of the ring and no referee calling break.

Certainly Scaith would see that he got to Switzerland. He could not afford to lose the Kimberly portfolio for British use. He would be stamped as a traitor if he let it go.

Kimberly wished he had time to deal with the other major powers. But, as things stood, it was better to carry through his present plans. Luck was riding with him. He still had a fair chance, a fifty-fifty chance if the K.G.B. failed to pick up his scent. A fifty-fifty chance was more than he had had many times before. He had never failed to come out smelling comparatively sweet until he had been forced to run to Moscow.

Commander Scaith must know it was he who had knocked out the cop but, in the face of the entire Metropolitan Police Force, he would defend him to the death. Defend him, at least, until he had the information he was buying in his hands. Then—ah, yes—then! Then it would be a different matter. But the cash would help. And Her Majesty's Chancellor would be obliged, willy-nilly, to unbelt.

When Kimberly reached Woburn village, he had already made some purchases and was confident he would no longer be singled out as a "toff." A pair of glasses helped to disguise his eyes. A muffler took the place of collar and tie. Beneath the raincoat, he was pleasantly paunchy once again, obviously a man who liked his beer. His head was covered by a jaunty flat tweed cap. Now it was up to him to watch his accent.

He pulled up at a village store and bought a paperback novel. In the post office he paid for a large registered envelope, put the book into it and addressed it to Robert Flemming, Poste Restante, Geneva, Switzerland. He put the postal receipt away carefully.

He drove through the village and turned into Woburn Abbey Park. He had heard of many changes and was anxious to see them for himself. Although half the Abbey had been demolished by the old Duke before he died, the remainder still constituted one of the largest stately homes in the British Isles.

During the war when the great house, stripped of its finery and patrolled by men in battle-dress, was occupied by M.1.5., he had spent long periods there, resting from expeditions in the field and conducting an extraordinarily facile double life. Here, strangely enough, he had always felt at peace. Even now, he was touched by a sense of arrival and achievement as he parked the car and bought a tourist ticket for the house. The big game was nearly over. He felt he was on the winning side. Yet, nothing must be left to chance. He had to observe everything himself before he talked to Scaith again.

What he needed was a foolproof place to leave a sample of his microfilm as barter for his safe conduct to Switzerland, unless he risked posting it to Scaith. The whole portfolio had been reduced in this way to a small packet no bigger than the book he had sent to Switzerland.

When he was finished with the house, he made a tour of the children's playground and the zoo and then, back in the car again, he patrolled the park. He was flagged by a keeper, advised to get a move on: the place was closing for the night, but he was satisfied. He had decided on the best way to get out if he was double-crossed and had to run. It would not be the first time he had misled the hounds. All that remained now was to get into the church.

It was already 6:30 but there were lights shining from within. Someone must be there. He left Penny's car outside a pub where people were gathering for the evening pint. He walked back through the graveyard, straight into the church. Two women were arranging flowers, another sweeping up. They looked at him with some surprise, but from early childhood he had been familiar with the drill: he lifted his cap to them, tucked it under his arm, slid into a back pew, and bowed his head in prayer. No one would disturb him there.

Through his fingers, he saw at once there were no changes in the church structure since his last visit. A pleasing air of timelessness pervaded, assimilating the ladies at their work, himself the man at prayer, and now the vicar who came through the vestry door behind the altar, wearing a tweed coat over his clerical cloth. It seemed to Kimberly they were all pieces of a huge jigsaw puzzle which would never be complete.

He saw the vicar glance in his direction, watched him walk to the main door and lock it, then go back to the ladies to admire their work. There was a little gentle laughter and, after a pause, they all three looked at him. Followed by the vicar to the side door, they called good-byes, three lilting refined farewells like bird song as they left.

The vicar returned alone. He was obviously waiting for Kimberly to bring his prayer to a conclusion before he left the church. As soon as Kimberly stood up, the vicar approached him, holding out his hand. "As you see, we are preparing for the great day: Good Friday and Easter weekend," he said. Kimberly took his hand, squeezed the fingers, found them to be hard as iron. "The culmination of Holy Week," the vicar continued, making himself more clear in case Kimberly had not understood.

"Ah, yes . . . the ascension into Heaven." Kimberly smiled. "Visually quite charming. Yet, the descent into Hell has got its picturesque appeal as well." He spoke with a soft Irish lilt. "I'd like to see some of my countrymen from the I.R.A. down there."

The vicar regarded him with curiosity. "Unhappily, Hell is considered somewhat out-of-date these days. But it is no good thing to wish anyone there. You're not from here?"

"No. Oh, I was here. A long time ago. In and out during the war." He gestured toward the park. "In there."

"Ah, then you've lost a lot of friends." It was not a question. He knew. "I was in the desert myself. Long time ago, as you said. But they were not truly bad days. We were . . ."

"Fighting for a better world?" Kimberly suggested.

"And we've got to go on doing it." The vicar edged him down the aisle. "Lovely spring weather it was today," he said as they reached the side door. He locked it and put the key under a convenient stone. "I leave it there for choir practice. We're attempting a rather special anthem for Good Friday: the young lads will be coming in for extra practice tonight. Cocoa and a bun thrown in."

"And what goes on during the normal week?"

"Well, I take matins at outlying places, and evensong in Dunstable. Quid pro quo, y'know: their vicar will preach here on Wednesday night but this Sunday is the big day. Please come along if you happen to be here."

In the open air, he could see that, in spite of his rotund stomach, the stranger looked drawn and ill. The vicar was disturbed. Although not one of his parishoners, the man had come into the church alone to pray. Was it not his duty to hold out a helping hand?

"Perhaps you would like to come back to the rectory with me for a chat? There is always something in the larder."

"No. I was just passing. Thanks all the same."

"Well, nice to have met you."

The vicar shook his hand firmly once again and walked away. Kimberly followed behind him but stopped at the pub and bought himself a drink and a ham sandwich. He then moved the car to a side street and walked back to the church.

He found the key beneath the stone where the vicar had left it and let himself in. It was dark inside. He waited until he grew accustomed to the gloom before crossing the nave and following the west aisle to where a niche housed a flying angel commemorating one of the ancient dead.

He produced a pencil-torch and screwdriver. It took some time to find the crack he was looking for. But, at last, he was able to insert the screwdriver and gently lever a chunk of marble out of place. He put his hand into the hole and retrieved his case of microfilm.

Although he had been confident of finding it, he was elated and relieved. He desperately wanted to light a cigarette, but an innate sense of propriety prevented him from smoking in church.

He moved to the nearest pew and sank onto the unrelenting oak. He breathed deeply, staring over the empty seats towards the altar, its silver palely gleaming, clinging to the last light from the multicoloured window above the crucifix.

There was little time to rest. The choirboys would be arriving any minute, faces scrubbed and hair slicked into place, to match their piping trebles to the organ pipes. Kimberly used his torch again, holding it between his teeth while he snipped a short length of celluloid from the rest. He tore a sheet out of a hymn book, wrapped the snippet carefully and stowed it in an inner pocket, along with the receipt of the registered package to Geneva. The remainder he replaced in its container. He considered taking the whole file with him, but second thoughts decided him to leave it where it had been in safety for so long.

Before leaving the church, he took an impression of the key in wax he had ready and malleable against his skin. He put the key back beneath its stone, lit a cigarette, and walked slowly back to Penny's car.

He knew his day was not nearly over yet.

Five

In London the papers still showed interest in the assault on Grierson, the footballing policeman. There were loud cries for vengeance. Football fans swarmed the towpath. The evening papers gave more information than the morning editions: a boat was found drifting toward Westminister. No one wanted to believe it had merely been badly moored. It was photographed as the getaway craft used by the thug. Business had seldom been better in the Putney pub.

By the afternoon, the Soviet Embassy leaked the news that the British were holding one of their staff in illegal and secret custody. The Foreign Office spokesman blandly denied the story.

Commander Scaith did not return to his office after lunch. He stayed in his own home, making personal calls to Press Barons and to the Heads of Departments of Police, begging discretion. But since he withheld explanation why the attack on this policeman should be handled differently from any other, they promised little co-operation and gave none. The very request for discretion impelled the newspapers to renew their inquiries. Something definitely smelt.

Scaith fumbled his way furiously into his top-coat. Time was when a request from a Commander Scaith was an order! But now—this new upstart brand of news editor—they must be put down! He stomped his way out onto the tow-path. Again, he leaned over the wall, focusing on the clutter of boats floating freely on the river in full flood. Slowly his calm was restored.

He repaced the territory he had covered the night before with the Russian. The police reports had told of the woman who had opened her window and seen someone running. He had called out, informing anyone who cared to listen that a man had gone over the wall into the boats. Then he had vanished. How had he vanished? Into the dark. Scaith pondered. It had not been dark last night. On the contrary, the moon was coming up for full.

Scaith had suggested James Chorley have the woman requestioned by a man from his own section.

"Ask if the man who called out was a foreigner," he had instructed. "If he had a heavy accent."

The news came back from Chorley's man: no accent. According to the lady at the window, the man who called out was a toff. And he had not vanished into the dark. In fact, it was she who had turned back into her room to fetch her husband to have a look. By the time she got back to the window, the man who had called out on the towpath had already gone. Gone where? Over the wall, she presumed, after the burglar, like a toff would. According to Chorley's man, the lady herself had a strong London accent. He doubted if she could tell a foreign accent from a Dublin one.

But a toff? Scaith pondered. That was a very special term. It had a meaning which could not be debased, a hallmark of its own. *Were* there two men? It must have been Sergei Kuzminsky who had run beneath the lady's window. Could he be instantly recognised, in moonlight, as springing from the top drawer? Could anyone? Scaith remembered Kuzminsky had a certain grace, a finesse of movement that told of discipline. But that could have been acquired in the army or on a football field. The lady, however, had based her verdict on his position in life entirely on his voice. In that split second it took for him to enter and leave her life, she had recognised an upper-class accent.

Scaith recalled the Russian speaking good, if pedantic, English but with a heavy foreign overtone. If, while running for his life, he had called out to promote a wild-goose chase among the boats, to lead Grierson that way and not behind the pub where he was knocked out, the lady should have known him for a foreigner at once.

But she could not be shaken in her conviction that the man was a toff.

"Could he have been a foreign toff?" Chorley's man had asked.

The lady knew of no such animal.

Commander Scaith stood for a long moment in deep thought. There seemed lessening room for doubt that Sergei Kuzminsky and the man who had called out were one and the same person. Could the man have been an Englishman? Or, perhaps, one of the upper crust from Central Europe who used to be educated only at the top English public schools before following up at Oxford or Cambridge? Such a man, living in Moscow, would have gravitated normally toward a Philip Kimberly and, more than likely, be numbered among his intimates. Such a man could easily adopt a phony foreign accent for his own purposes but, on the run, forget it momentarily.

He turned abruptly and went home to telephone the Scotsman in charge of the Fingerprint Section of New Scotland Yard.

Prints had been found on the mahogany armrests of the chair in Milroy's office. Since office personnel had been eliminated, and no one else had used the chair, they had to be read as the prints of the missing Russian.

"Gude prints," said the Scotsman with a strong accent. "We have the left hand and fingers perfectly. A gude broad hand. The right is a wee bitty smudged."

"Have they been computer-run?"

"Aye. No trace. But they will i.d. the mon, and no mistake. when we lay hands on him."

"Run them against every foreign print we have. All the way back. Poles we used as agents during the war. Especially the ones escaping the Germans through Russia. Some of them saved their skins by selling out to the Russkies and then were filtered into *our* networks to double. We blew a lot of them but there were hundreds. Run the prints we have from the prison camps, soldiers we picked up in the Berlin shambles. Some of them were planted."

"Aye, sir. I'll carry on. Perrfect prints to work on."

Scaith further advised him to run the files on foreign dignitaries, famous people who, with or without their knowledge, had been printed for security and positive identification in case of bomb damage or mutilation or kidnapping.

"Diplomats, yachtsmen, Generals, missing files, war correspondents. All the top foreigners we have. And cover the British as well. Although, I'll lay odds our man comes from east of Calais."

"Aye!" the Scot agreed. "That is where the difference starts!"

His *r*'s rolled more aggressively than usual in defence of the White Cliffs, not to mention Hadrian's Wall.

Penny's train arrived in London at Paddington Station. She bought herself a pack of cigarettes and an evening paper. She saw a free taxi approaching, going in the right direction, and signalled it. In spite of Kimberly's warning, she had decided to nip quickly into her flat and pick up a change of clothes. She gave her address, leant into the corner of the cab and opened the newspaper. The headlines were enough: "MISS-ING RUSSIAN DIPLOMAT!"

She leaned forward and tapped the glass between herself and the driver. Why take any risks? She gave the address of Farquar's flat. And, in this way, she missed the unexpected visit of her girlfriend, Susan Peters.

Susan had had no time to telephone. Luck had struck too unexpectedly. She had found herself free of all her obligations for the night. She ran to Penny's flat, hurrying breathlessly through the door and tapping her small foot impatiently as the lift carried her to Penny's floor. She scarcely noticed the man who rode up with her and continued to the next landing.

Susan was in love. Already she was mentally involved in the long night ahead to be spent in the blissfully squeaky bed with Ginger in his rooming house. But first she had to square it with Penny in case her mother phoned.

She leant on Penny's bell, leant harder, but still with no reply. She remembered Penny often left her key under the corner of the mat for the cleaning woman. She looked frenziedly. It was there. She let herself in to leave the vital note for Penny.

The man who had been with her in the lift

had returned to the ground floor and was already helping a companion carry a roll of carpet from a green van across the road into the building and into the lift.

At Penny's floor, they slid the unwieldy bundle to her door and rang the bell. Susan Peters answered it. The carpet fell toward her, forcing her back into the flat. The men walked in.

Scarcely minutes later, they returned downstairs. The odd-job man was at the door.

"Wrong address," the delivery man complained.

They moved off to stow the carpet in the small green van. The van left at once.

A Russian plane carried Boris Medvedev back to Moscow to report in person how he had let Kimberly-Kuzminsky get away. His dreams of seeing the Tower of London and Windsor Castle, of eating the strange English bangers Philip had always talked about, faded. He searched his memory for prayers.

His back to the setting sun, gilding the country he was leaving, over a grim Sweden and the darkening wastes of Poland, he was carried reluctantly. No one spoke to him. Nobody offered him refreshment. He was guilty of something. Guilt rubs off, contaminates. Far better to leave it alone. It could carry an infection for which there is no cure.

During the flight, Boris dreamed small dreams. In one, Kimberly turned up again with the missing documents, the hero dazzling the Kremlin with his reason for cutting away, Boris himself sharing the glory. All was forgiven but, unfortunately. hunger woke him.

Boris had a strange conviction that if Kimberly had been allowed to travel in his own guise, not mutilated. all would have been well. He had hated the transformation of his drunken, well-covered friend into the lean and destructive Slav. The old Kimberly would never have let him down this way. He had to remind himself that the old Kimberly was well and truly dead. He dozed again and thought he heard someone cry out. But only once. Perhaps that, too, was part of a bad dream.

In his flat, waiting for Penny, Farquar moved a potted plant from one table to another. He surveyed it from two different angles and moved it back again. He was forced to admit that Penny's L-shaped flat had much more warmth and welcome in it than his bachelor abode.

A picture of his mother stood on a console table. looking as remote as she had always looked throughout his childhood. Only once, when he was going to his public school for the first term, had she embraced him, saying, "Harry, Harry, I love you so very much, but it's wrong to tell boys that they are loved."

He picked up the photograph now and rubbed the glass against his coat in case his daily woman had forgotten to dust it properly. He set it back in place. He had an insane idea that she might break out again, shatter the glass, and tell him it was perfectly all right for a man to declare his love for a woman, however much a mother must keep it from her son.

He loved Penny. He was sure of it. With Kimberly's death, he had been prepared to offer her a change in their relationship, ask for a discharge from Scaith and hope that she might marry him.

Now, however, the Russian defector purporting to have documents once stolen by Philip Kimberly, and his assignment to James Chorley, put a temporary stop to any new plans. But they would catch the fellow soon. Penny need never know. The Russian would either be shipped back to his compatriots or locked quietly away.

He swallowed an enormous pink gin. There was no reason why the honeymoon should not begin tonight. At least he would propose. He began going over the words. He rushed into his bedroom and changed his tie for one she had admired a year ago. He came back and moved the potted plant again. He had just pushed the sofa to a place it had never been before when he heard her ring.

She behaved like an excited puppy when he let her in. She dropped her handbag and embraced him frantically. She hugged and kissed him many times. She put her fingers in his hair and ruffled it.

"Oh, Farq, Farq, Farq!"

He was extremely pleased. "Why, what's this all about?"

"Farq, Farq, I love you and you've got to marry me. You simply must. If you don't like it after forty years, I'll agree to a divorce. But we've got to do it soon!" So much for his proposal. "Well? Will you?"

"*I promessi sposi*," he said pontifically.

Penny laughed happily.

"That's *my* profession. Translations sixpence extra."

She moved away into the sitting room. Her past life was over, particularly the last two days. The next few would soon be gone. She turned and held out her arms to him.

"Hold me." He did. "Harry, Harry, I love you so very much."

Over her shoulder, he glimpsed his mother's photograph. Penny had never called him Harry before. The lady in the photograph would never seem remote again.

As soon as he let her go, she moved the sofa back to where it had always been. "Who's been pushing our furniture around?" she asked.

He began to laugh and then they both laughed. They each had something they were protecting the other from, but nothing was going to spoil things for them now. Farquar decided they were going to celebrate. Push out the boat.

"I have nothing to wear. My hair is in a mess." She gestured, the eternal female, hands bereft. "No clothes."

"The scrubbed look has come to stay," he said. "You scrub in the bath while I fix the celebration cup."

Half an hour later, she came back from the bathroom, swathed in a big towel, one shoulder bare, as were her feet.

Farquar stared. "You look so bloody lovely, it seems a pity to gild the lily. But try these on for size. Hold out your hands."

He emptied a chamois pouch into her gathered palms. She gasped and walked to the looking-glass above the fireplace.

I am going to turn into a doting fool, he told himself as he watched her putting on his mother's jewellery. When it was all done—neck, ears, wrists, fingers all adorned—she turned and let the towel drop around her feet, but it was not a sexual gesture. She looked extraordinarily pure. She touched the jewellery, compassion filtering through her smile.

"Farq, my darling Farq. When we get divorced in forty years, I'll give it back to you and, naturally, I'll give you the custody of all the children, too. I'll still be young—only sixty-two —but you'll be past it . . . poor old Farq." She kissed him on the nose, gave him a small push. "Go shave. Then we will go and mix with the lovely people and show them us while we're still on fire."

Farquar called the night Duty Officer at Central Office to let them know he would be at the Mirabelle in case he was needed. He added he was dining with a lady and would prefer to be undisturbed, except by Commander Scaith. He had news for him.

"Understood, sir," said the Duty Officer dryly. "I'll pass on your order to H.Q. and to the Prime Minister at once."

In spite of having nothing but the clothes she had turned up in, Penny managed to look glamorous. She had left off the shirt she had worn all day under a sleeveless dark grey flannel pinafore dress. One long row of pearls around her neck and another twisted in her hair had transformed the day look into evening dress.

Farquar kissed her shoulder. "I can see you're going to be cheap to clothe."

"All you need is enough jewellery." She kissed him back. "Which ring would you like me to be engaged with?"

Farquar insisted she must have a new one of her own. He told her he had booked a table at the Mirabelle and hoped she didn't mind.

"A concession to old age. That's me," he said. "We'll have a decent dinner there, fine wine, and then I'll take you somewhere to hop and skip and jump."

They had a drink to get them on their way and set off in Farquar's car. He asked where she had left hers.

First lie, she thought, as she told him she had left it in the country, deciding to take the train down. Then she realised it was really the truth and felt much happier.

"Good idea. You'd better lose that dangerous car."

"I love my car."

"You need a Mini."

"I don't want a Mini."

"A nice, shiny red one. A Cooper, even."

"Well . . . ummm . . . Cooper . . . perhaps."

"You're such an easy girl to please."

"I know."

As they walked through to the restaurant, Farquar saw Chorley occupying the best part of two seats in the inside bar. Chorley raised his eyes from a large whisky. The eyes swept past Farquar and settled appreciatively on Penelope. He sipped his drink, put his glass down, and waved a tiny wave.

Bastard! Farquar thought. Waiting for him all day, but the minute I don't want him, he's after me!

He hurried Penny through the bar.

"What's up?" Penelope asked.

"Hungry," Farquar said. "Let's set to."

He was suddenly ill at ease. To cover his abstraction, he forced himself to give more attention than usual to the menu. They ordered *homard au safran* with a chilled bottle of Montrachet, smiled at each other, and agreed that, because they were lusty eaters, the *côtelettes d'agneau* was the only sensible dish to follow.

"And the wine will do for that, too," she suggested providently.

He said, "I should hope so," but first ordered

two dry martinis to follow those they had had at home.

The ordering over, Farquar's attention drifted. Their conversation did not flow as easily as it had before. He seemed absorbed, but not by Penny.

Chorley's table, when he came in from the bar, was near enough to theirs for him to look archly at Penny throughout the meal. She pulled Farquar back from his daydreaming.

"That man who waved when we came in?"

"Umm?"

"Wake up, Farq! He's sitting just behind, over your right shoulder. Who is he?"

"Chorley. Sir James Chorley."

"A baronet?"

"No. He was knighted some time ago."

"What for?"

Farquar was vague.

"Services . . . something . . . made himself conspicuous."

"You don't get knighted just for making yourself conspicuous."

"Depends on who you've been conspicuous with."

"He looks quite interesting."

"I gather he finds you interesting, too."

Penelope looked back to Chorley's table and gave him a small smile. Farquar ate slowly, dragging out his meal. He tortured his cutlets, scarcely tasting them. He hoped he might have a brief word with Chorley in the gents on their way out, if he timed things carefully.

Penelope pointed to his plate. "You aren't liking your good grub."

"I think I over-ordered."

"But you were hungry."

"The lobster killed my appetite. Some lobsters do that."

"I've gone through the lot. Makes me look like a beast."

"Only because you are."

She laughed, and for a few minutes they were en rapport.

They were ordering coffee, the wine waiter hovering, pushing liqueurs, when Chorley came over to them. Farquar made a token gesture of standing up to welcome him, which Chorley ignored. He had leaned across the table, extending his hand to Penelope.

"The beautiful Miss Who?" he asked. She found herself shaking hands with him. Chorley crooked his finger to a waiter. "Chair," he commanded. "And bring my bill here. I'll sign." And only then did he turn to Farquar. "Well, old man, this is very nice of you. Yes, I'll have a Kummel, just to keep you company . . . and now you must introduce me to your friend."

"So sorry," Farquar apologised. "This is my fiancée, Miss—"

"Fiancée! Well! I didn't know," Chorley cut in.

"Kimberly," Penny said. "Penelope Kimberly."

"Kimberly?" Chorley's eyes, pale as glass marbles, questioned. "You did say Kimberly?"

Penny nodded, pushed a small smile, determined to play it right. She had been waiting for the first time she used her new old name.

"Yes. I am the daughter of the man who died the day before yesterday in Moscow."

It seemed such a short time ago and, cold as ice, deep in her heart, she knew it would have been better if Philip Kimberly had really died in Moscow. She took a long draught of wine, emptying her glass.

Farquar poured her more. He knew it must have been an effort on her part to acknowledge Philip Kimberly just now. But he did not know the full extent of the effort it had been.

Suddenly James Chorley was benign, kindly, full of concern for her. "Poor child. No good pretending I don't know all about Philip Kimberly. Perhaps, since he had been away so long, the blow was not as painful as if he had been with you all the time. I am so sorry, my dear girl. I hope the newspapers haven't bothered you."

"They tried. I ran away. To friends."

"You ran away. How wise. Did you go far?"

"Far enough."

"And you will be going back to your friends tonight?"

Penelope thought James Chorley was probably too old-fashioned to appreciate a girl living with her fiance before marriage.

"In the early hours." She leaned across to Farquar. "We're out to celebrate tonight. No good pretending I am broken up. Although Philip . . ."

She paused. "My father was a damned nice man to have known years ago."

"So I have heard, so I have heard. . . ."

A waiter called Farquar to the telephone. He excused himself. It was Commander Scaith. His voice was caustic.

"You are doing yourself proud."

"A decent dinner, sir, now and then."

"May I ask who you are dining with?"

"I am with Sir James Chorley, sir."

"Are you, indeed? And who else? A table of three, I am told."

"Penelope. Miss Kimberly."

"Very cosy. Reminiscing about her old dad, eh?"

"No, sir."

"I am surprised. He was a close friend of Chorley's. Anyway, neither here nor there. You've been leaving call-back messages for me. What's the news?"

"The news is—and the Met Police have it, too: their source is the same as mine—they might have a lead to the Russian. A whore in Soho. She's been chatting about some wounded man with slanting eyes. But when they questioned her, she dried up at once."

"The honour of a prostitute. Inspiring, ain't it?"

"Very, sir. I've been round to see her: Clara Dredge, 6 Barwell Street, Soho. But, unhappily, she has a regular customer who sends a car for her every Wednesday at five o'clock. Won't be back until tomorrow morning."

"Lucky little Clara Dredge," Scaith said, mentally shuffling through his index of friends who were incommunicado every Wednesday night.

"I may get something from her the chaps in uniform couldn't dig up."

"Make sure it ain't something you can't get rid of. And if you take your pants off, don't charge it to expenses. You think there might be something in this?"

"I'll be with Miss Dredge first thing tomorrow morning."

"Do that. We must find Kuzminsky before he falls to the Met Police. They'll either lynch him, or some clot will shoot him by accident. No one must lay hands on him but us. Understood?"

"Understood, sir."

"The Russians are making an almighty fuss about the blighter. They know he's on the crook. They've already had one shot at him. Bet they're beginning to regret old Kimberly. He'd never have played a dirty trick like this on them."

"Kimberly, yes." Farquar paused. "Actually, sir, I am going to marry Miss Kimberly. I'll be asking to leave the Service when this is over."

"You will, will you? Well, let me tell you something: I don't give a damn! Sex, sex—all the bloody time!"

Farquar heard Scaith slam his receiver down hard. He chuckled softly, aware of a supreme sense of freedom sweeping over him as he announced his imminent departure from the Service.

He returned to his table to find Penelope hysterical with laughter. Chorley got up to leave at once.

"Miss Kimberly finds me funny. *Au revoir*, my dear young lady. I hope to be able to amuse you as much another day." He made a little dart forward to finger her pearls. "Lovely. Really lovely. So rare these days. Everything else is fake and false. Mark my words."

He bobbed his head to Farquar, murmured something that sounded like "night-night" and left. Penny was still hilarious.

"That is the strangest man I ever did meet."

"I know he says outrageous things but what was so funny? Specially?"

"Don't make me repeat it now. I'll tell you later. He's bonkers. *Vraiment* bonkers!"

Her laugh was infectious. Farquar found himself chuckling by her side.

"What will you take to match his Kummel?"

"Completely mad!" she said. "Anything he takes is good enough for me. Maybe it's the Kummel that does it!" Farquar ordered two Kummels and she saw the waiter smiling as they went back to holding hands. "We got engaged today," she confided.

The waiter congratulated them and soon the *maître d'hôtel* presented himself at their table to offer more Kummels on the house.

When Farquar had paid enormously and they were sitting in his car, she moved in closer.

"I don't really have to go back to the country to my friends and I don't really think I could hop and skip and jump tonight."

"Shall we go home?"

"Absolutely nowhere else!"

Six

Kimberly left Woburn behind and turned towards Oxford. He was making for a place some miles outside the university town: a stretch of farmland like a wedge of Camembert cheese, pasture on the two longer sides and a wood breaking the north wind on a slightly higher level at the thick end of the wedge. Here, in this nicely sheltered pastoral setting, Professor Piers Purloe had been fortunate to set up house some forty years ago and had reigned there ever since.

Kimberly knew every corner of the miniature estate, every pathway through the woods and every track across the fields which grassed the professorial cows. He drove slowly round the well-remembered slice of land. All aspects of the charming Queen Anne house were pleasing. Night had settled gently. The moon, which had been filling out the night before, was rising again in a pale, cloudless sky, bright enough to throw shadows like giant flowerpots beneath the meadow trees. He had rarely seen the place so lovely.

When he arrived back at the finger-post pointing from the main road, he decided, because of the brightness of the night, it would be safer to drive round again until he reached the wood. He would look for a pull-in where one might expect to find a courting couple, and park there rather than on the open road. Plenty of students from the university would be looking for privacy on a night like this, with nothing but an old car like Penny's between themselves and the crowd. It was the best plan.

He continued slowly up the slight hill towards the wood, found the perfect place, backed the car in under low-hanging beech leaves and switched off the lights. He took Penny's shotgun out of the boot and moved off through the wood in the direction of the house.

It was downhill, a gentle slope all the way until the trees thinned out. At the fringe of the wood, he halted. He looked out over an open space between himself and a range of farm buildings serving the house of Professor Purloe, the Chief Recruiting Officer and Paymaster of the Soviet Union in Great Britain.

Kimberly wondered if the man had changed as little as the house. It was possible. He had always seemed older than his years. His pedantic mind and his scholarly approach to life, the reverence with which Youth waited for his words, made a

Moses out of him before his time, and Kimberly had been his Aaron.

There was only one light in the rear of the house. There had always been only one light. The world-famous professor of history lived alone. A man came in to milk his cows and tend the lawns, and women walked through the fields from the village daily to dust and wash and cook. At times, favoured students were invited to a lusty cold supper laid in the big kitchen on the plain boards. Sometimes they had been known to stay till dawn.

Gentle austerity befitting a savant moulded his way of life, though from time to time he gave a dinner party in great style: damask and crystal, fine food, and college servants drawn in willingly to frame their famous man in a dignity which was spoken of with envy by other scholars in distant lands. In season, a roasted swan, neck wired and head tucked beneath a wing, was often the main dish.

As a youth, Kimberly had eaten the cold kitchen fare, idolising Purloe, hanging on his words. As a grown man, he had many times partaken of the swan. The last time had been more than ten years ago. Since then he had lived a different life. He had visited the Citadel, walked the Kremlin corridors, been to the source, seen it all.

Kimberly stood quite still, studying the house. He knew that Piers Purloe would have been informed of the true identity of the Russian subject who had broken away at London airport and was still at large. He could already have been issued with a copy of the new passport photograph. One thing was certain: the Russian Embassy in London could expect that Kimberly might return to his old haunts where he might possibly have hidden the stolen goods at the very seat of his theft. In any case, a guard would have been installed to protect the famous Englishman who was the safest secret link between the Kremlin and the West.

More than an hour went by before Kimberly saw the guard. Nothing could have looked more native to the pastoral scene. This was no thug loitering on the smooth academic lawn. This man, of stocky build, wore good country clothes and carried a sporting gun, presumably to frighten poachers rather than kill sleeping birds at night. He fitted the picture perfectly, but not so his dog: an evil-looking Alsatian, slinking at his heels. Kimberly wondered in what way the shotgun had been modified to kill a man and not a bird in flight. He hoped he would find out the easy way, knowing he had no cartridges himself.

The guard and the dog made the tour around the house, then took the path leading to the flower garden and the pool where Kimberly had so often swum. He then felt free to move, streaking silently across the open grass in the direction the man and dog had gone.

He heard them up ahead of him, probing the shrubbery. He took ten quick strides and was hidden beside a rustic summerhouse once used for dressing by the pool. Now was the moment to entice the dog. He only had to snap a twig. A moment later, the snarling animal was through the hedge and at him like a thunderbolt, teeth bared viciously and ready for his throat. With mechanical precision, Kimberly dropped onto his knees, let the gun fall, and raised his arms. He broke the neck of the dog as it sailed over him, somersaulting into the pool with a soft splash, quite dead.

Once more, Kimberly was a dark shadow against the moss-covered wood on the dark side of the summerhouse. Everything was dark. He smelled wet rot oozing from the timbers. The same smell had lent a weird excitement to an hour he had spent there with his naked wife the first summer before they married. She had been erotic with excitement meeting Purloe: an ardent communist kissing the prophet's hem. After that, she was all Kimberly's, no holding back. She and he were one. Their engagement was announced the next day. How long would a rustic summerhouse moulder and remain erect? he wondered. How long would a crumbling world take to disintegrate?

The guard had come back, whistling for his dog. He had heard the splash and was now at his most vulnerable, bending over the pool.

Kimberly stepped forward, weight on his left foot, and swung his right leg with full force. The point of his shoe connected with the crouching man's temple and carried him into the pool beside the dog. His shotgun slithered down the ladder and into the pool as Kimberly bent to pick it up. It was gone. No chance now to investigate what a corrupt and clever gunsmith might have done with it.

The man surfaced, arms flaying the water ineffectually, shouting in Russian for help. It was evident he could not swim even to the shallow end.

Kimberly held out a long, aluminium pole used for cleaning the swimming pool. He enticed the man, encouraging him in his own language towards the steps. There, he landed him and knocked him out. He trussed him up with garden wire from a shed and gagged him. He hid him in the summerhouse and removed his own provisional disguise, rolling everything into his coat to be used again. He went back to the house, depositing his bundle on the well-kept lawn.

A light shone from the windows further down the wall. He used the butt of his gun and his foot to break into the study. The old man had no time to find his revolver before Kimberly crushed his fingers with his own.

"Piers," he said. "Forgive me for dropping in without a word." Still holding Piers Purloe's hand, he leaned across and found the gun and released the bony fingers. He tossed the gun into an armchair and stood back. "That is how I always like to think of you: aloof, cut off from the common herd, no one daring to approach the venerable man."

He saw Piers Purloe throw a desperate glance toward the Georgian windows, searching the lawns beyond for help that should be there. Kimberly shook his head and made a gesture with both his hands of wiping a slate clean.

He crossed to a corner cupboard, opened it, lifted the stopper from a crystal decanter, sniffed the neck, and poured a brimming drink. He sipped it as he sank into a comfortable chair. The whole performance had been like a meticulously rehearsed dance. He put his glass beside him on a stool and forced Piers Purloe's eyes to meet his own.

"Well, Piers," he said. "You really haven't changed at all. The years have passed you by." He smiled briefly. "But I've a feeling they will stop tonight."

A small bubble of saliva appeared on the professor's lips. He tapped it gently with a neatly folded silk handkerchief. His voice was a whisper of unbelief.

"Yes . . . you *are* Kimberly."

"What is left of him." He held up his scarred hand. "You do remember the mark of Cain? The Comrade Surgeon overlooked it when they decided to emulate Comrade Frankenstein. But, as they snipped and sewed, they slipped up somewhere. That fat, amiable, good-eating and big drinking man was totally destroyed. They took a vital part out of the jigsaw and left a mean and bitter man. Vengeful and self-seeking."

"What do you want with me?"

"For a start, passports. Whatever you have available. Remember how expert I always was at processing them? And, of course, I will need money."

"I have very little money here. Things have changed."

"Not in the last few months. I died only two days ago, remember? I was still a Hero of the Soviet Union. Cross of Stalin. I know what has and what hasn't changed, old boy." Kimberly crossed the room, manipulated a spring, and folded back a triple shelf of books concealing another triple set of shelves. "Passports: male," he said, examining a bundle. "Swedish, Irish Free State, Jugoslav. Yes, I could be Jugoslav the way they've fixed me up. And anyone can look Irish if he's drunk enough." He selected those he wanted, put the others back, and closed the bookshelves with a click. "You see, Piers? No trouble, no disarray." He picked up the revolver, checked the breech. "Loaded. Good. Now, the money."

"You'll pay for this, Kimberly. You know you will."

"I daresay. We all pay in the end." He took Purloe's arm into a tight lock behind his back, swinging him round. "You are just beginning." He pushed him towards a Chinese Chippendale screen, kicked it aside, and pulled Purloe up facing a large old-fashioned safe. "Where the old man keeps his goodies. His C.B.E., his *Légion d'Honneur*, his Southern Cross, all the trophies of a most successful life. Open it."

Piers Purloe manipulated the dials and swung open the heavy iron door. He stood erect, watching Kimberly stow neatly bundled packets of money into his pockets.

"You are a disgrace to the cause we have worked for selflessly," Purloe said.

Suddenly Kimberly strode forward and struck Purloe across the face with the barrel of the revolver. His voice trembled in a whisper of repressed rage. "Don't speak to me of cause or disgrace. You've sat here surrounded by your comforts all your life, nibbling on Stilton cheese, savouring wines, sending—count, Piers, start counting!—how many gloriously enthusiastic young people have you sent into a battle they could in no way comprehend, corrupting and wasting lives? You bloodless man! While the world dies, gagging on its own dishonour, have you spent years in a Russian prison? Or an English one? You smug, self-satisfied bastard! Of course, I stole your files! All your lovely microfilm: the source of all your lovely power over so many lovely people. That microfilm was to be a passport for my wife. To join me in Russia. A passport even the K.G.B. wouldn't dispute. And she *would* have joined me, Purloe. But for you! Even though she was hemmed in by Special Branch in Switzerland, I would have got someone through to smuggle her out. But you were terrified. You could see her only as an immediate threat: the British might break her, expose you, your entire organisation. And someone *did* get through to Annabelle: perhaps a foreign journalist with a message of comfort from her dear old friend, the kind professor. A messenger she received gladly. In the privacy of her own rooms. And it was that messenger who pushed her through that high window in Lausanne!"

"No! Never! She—"

"Committed suicide? Why? I was safe. Cradled in the welcoming arms of Mother Russia. She had everything to live for, waiting only to join me. But you had her killed, Purloe. And you slept again, secure on your fine goosefeather pillows. And all these years, all these years I had to swallow that knowledge and live with it, always smiling, always silent. Then they decided: I must bring the precious files back to Moscow. And never was there a more willing traveller than myself. I came to England to kill you."

Kimberly calmly raised the revolver and fired one bullet between Professor Piers Purloe's eyes He spat on the body, kicked open the windows, and went out. He found his bundle on the lawn and hurried through the woods.

Utterly weary, utterly disgusted, he drove back through a sleeping, moonlit England to the Bull Hotel.

Seven

In the heart of England, in London town, Penny stirred in Farquar's bed. They nuzzled each other like two sleeping pups. At times, they made small, contented sounds in place of words, a few words sometimes breaking through and fading back to sounds and deeper sleep and from the edge of sleep a small chuckle from Penny with an undertone of grief. She had lost her dream of Kimberly: he was changed, gone for good, lost to her. She was no longer Kimberly's kid. But she was Farquar's girl. And that fool . . . in the restaurant . . . what had he said? She laughed.

Farquar woke. Nerves which had been totally relaxed coiled again. "Sshhh. You'll wake the mice. What is it?"

"Nothing, nothing . . ." she murmured in half-sleep. "That old Chorley fellow . . . imagine . . . imagine . . . saying you were queer . . . darling faggy Farq . . ."

145

Farquar's reaction was of complete surprise. "Did he, hum?"

"With a fellow called Paul Ives."

He put his hand in her hair, feeling the silk, caressing her skull. "Sleep, darling . . . sleep."

And, like an obedient child, she did.

Farquar was ice-cold with rage. But it was more than rage. He felt a tinge of fear. The Paul Ives file was closed. It was over for Ives: a little compassion from his friends, and that was it. In the game of crime and punishment, he had evened up, set the price on his own head, and paid. What was James Chorley doing, bringing up his name? Suggesting to Penelope? Must be more to it than a stupid sexual joke in the most regrettable taste. Surely unlike Chorley. What?

"Poor Paul Ives." He said it again and again to himself. "Poor Paul."

It had destroyed his sleep. He eased himself gently out of bed, picked up his dressing gown, and shut the door on Penny.

He turned a light on in the sitting room and wheeled out an ornate lacquered cabinet. Fastened with a combination lock, it held his filing system. He slid the numbers into sequence: twenty-five, the last letter of the alphabet but one, a Y. Sixteen was P, nineteen for S, and number nine for the ninth letter, I. This added up to YPSI. Reversed, it became I SPY: childish, but even now it made him smile.

He pulled out his file on Paul Ives to tidy it off. He wrote Dead, the date and, in brackets,

146

suicide, Hotel Plaza, New York. He slid it back into place.

After the I's came J. He had a Joshua who had sent spies into Jericho in biblical times. These were the ones he liked. Delilah, for instance. He was fond of her, out there in the field spying for the Philistines. And, amongst the F's, there was Foley, the first recognised industrial spy. It was Farquar's hobby. He had a vague idea of publishing one day, when he could find time to write a scholarly book.

Farquar decided to close the Kimberly file as well. He did so, giving the information from the obituary in the *Times*: Cirrhosis of the liver. Scaith's voice came across his thoughts: "aggravated by a bloody bullet in the liver." Perhaps Scaith was right. In pencil this time, and between brackets, he wrote *Murdered?* with the question mark. Anyway, the man was dead, and Penny Kimberly would soon be Mrs. Farquar. He would give his filing cabinet to old Commander Scaith as his farewell present from the Service: a full stop and a new chapter for Penny and himself. This was his last assignment.

To refresh his memory on details of Sir James Chorley before locking up his box of tricks, he slid out the Chorley file. Chorley's was a success story all the way. From grammar school, he had won a scholarship to Oxford where he read law, achieving a double first. When he came down, a small inheritance had allowed him to travel for some time before joining a firm of London attorneys. The firm prospered. A certain flamboyance in their handling of divorce achieved them notoriety and wealthy clients. Chorley, jockeying for position as the more conservative partners retired, was now head of the firm.

It was the perfect cover for his true métier as the spider of all Spy Catchers, instinct uncanny, nose infallible. Farquar told himself he was lucky to have this last opportunity of getting to know Chorley before he married and moved on to a more prosaic life. He was going to take Penny right away: a bus to Katmandu. He locked up and went back to bed. Perhaps she wouldn't want to go by bus? Her warmth crept over him. He felt elated.

It was going to be good.

Penny woke at eight. She put on Farquar's pyjama jacket and his slippers and shuffled to the kitchen.

"What are you up to?" he called to her.

"Ministering to the master."

"I'll accept that. Make mine a four-minute egg."

She filled the kettle and put china on the kitchen table. She heard the plop of letters falling from the letter box at the front door. She went to fetch them.

Farquar came in, half-dressed in dark trousers and shirt, a club tie dangling in his fingers.

"Very fetching," he said. He picked up the tail of his pyjama coat hanging round her hips and fondled her bottom. "Do you know why women are the only female animal who have bosoms permanently filled, as opposed to all the other mammary females, who only fill out when they need to feed their young?" He told her the reason while he knotted his tie. "Evidently, when the human animal had still walked on all fours, the male had followed the swelling rumps of the lady who appealed to him."

Penny smiled, listened vaguely, looked expectant, waiting for the end. But her mind was wandering, already preoccupied with her day's work.

"So you see," Farquar continued, "when the bewitching female finally stood up on two legs and walked around, she had to provide permanently those two sweet bumps her mate had been so keen on following. Nice!"

He put his two hands under the pyjama jacket. She lay against his chest. He sensed she was not involved in his caress.

"Abstract," he said. "You are far away."

"Darling! Just trying to conjugate in four languages. I have a heavy day: Wogs and Frogs, Huns and goddamn English, all selling hotel equipment to each other, and one of them is going to pinch my bottom, so I'm preoccupied about trying to protect my rump. And bumps. Let go!"

"Reluctantly. And, what's more, you didn't plug the kettle in."

They went into the kitchen. He took the news-

149

paper from her, glanced at the headlines. He was preoccupied himself but neither of them wanted it to show. Yet, between them, they forgot the eggs.

Farquar gave her spare keys, apologised that he could not give her lunch, and said he'd phone her about dinner.

"I'll get some food," she said. "We'll have dinner at home."

"Nicely domestic."

He loitered in the doorway.

"That's the way it's going to be," she said.

He went to the lift. Penny waved. He hesitated.

"Better dress before my charlady arrives. I fear she would be shocked."

Penny shook her head in disbelief. "How can you be so old and know so little about life. Your charlady has been trying to get me to move in here for well over a year!"

The lift arrived.

"Can't be true!"

"True!"

Farquar vanished into the lift.

Penny dressed and telephoned the Bull Hotel. Pauline Ransom answered her. Penny told her she was not to worry about her friend's bill. She would take care of it.

"Tell him just to leave the car. I'm rather busy for a few days. He'll understand." She sighed deeply to herself. "Tell him I phoned."

"Don't worry about your friend," Pauline said cheerfully. "Doug heard him come in late last night. About one o'clock. I was sound asleep but he came down at eight this morning. Seems to be in the money. Paid up what Doug gave you. Was very nice. Said he'd like to spend tonight but he'd managed to settle his problem. Money, money! Christ, what a bore it is! He must have seen—"

"Yes," Penny interrupted. "Must have seen his —solicitor. Well, that's all right. Where is he now?"

"Gone out."

"I'm awfully grateful to you, Pauline. You and Doug."

"That's all right, duck. See you when you pick up your car. Amazes me how that wagon of yours keeps going!"

"Nothing wrong with my old wagon. 'Bye."

Penny was relieved. Philip hadn't got gangrene or septicaemia or he wouldn't have gone out. She did not understand where Philip had got money. Maybe he had sold her gun. She knew that it was valuable. He must have given it to her mother.

For a moment, she was caught in a web of yesterday. Her parents, those two tall, lovely people looking down at her, telling her so seriously never to point a gun at anyone . . . dead and gone . . . dead and gone. . . .

But Philip was not dead and gone. He was back again to love and admire. Admire? She questioned herself. To help, in any case. She had done everything she could. With the ruthlessness of youth, she reassured herself she had. Later everything would be all right. Yes. Later. It would all be sorted out. There would be time for friendship to flourish between them. Yes, like the old days. She tried to bury the knowledge that the old days were gone for good.

Now, it was time for her to leave. She needed money for herself, and that meant the bank before work.

She hurried.

Penny was unaware of being followed both to her bank and afterwards to the Dorchester Hotel. Soon she became totally involved in her day's work.

When Philip Kimberly left the Bull Hotel, he took Penny's car and drove to a side road where he resumed his yesterday's disguise. Now that he had money, he would improve on his altered appearance. He continued into town and, since it was early, easily found a place to park in the main street.

He bought a small packet of writing paper, envelopes and a ball-point pen. He decided to take the train to London as Penny had done the day before. His telephone call to Scaith would be anonymous from there.

He bought a town coat and a trilby hat and a more expensive pair of glasses and he went into the chemist shop to get something to relieve his pain. The wound was giving him hell again. It was the same shop Penny had used to buy his razor the day before. Today a young girl was serving. She was consulting with the chemist in the rear of the shop. He had only just arrived and was busy changing into his working coat.

Kimberly asked for water. The girl gave him a small medicine glass to swallow down his pills.

"Only two," she warned him. "No more until late afternoon. Hope they do you good."

Kimberly nodded his thanks. The chemist came forward as he was leaving. He saw Kimberly get into the car. He chatted to his assistant.

"That's the car the girl with the tooth abscess had. Good cars, they were. Must be ten years old. Pain killers, was it? Matter of fact, I went round to the Bull myself for a pint last night just to have another look at her."

"Oh, you are a devil, Mr. Brown. Lucky I'm your daughter's friend, or you'd be after me, eh?"

She dodged behind the counter. He looked at her over his spectacles.

"Man can't help his nature, my dear."

Another early customer came in needing laxatives and advice. He was given both.

Again Kimberly found a secluded spot to change into his city coat, his dark felt hat and horn-rimmed spectacles. If it were not for the throbbing of his arm, he would have felt supremely confident. He wrapped up the few inches of microfilm giving data on an important Cabinet Minister, put it in an envelope and printed Scaith's address, then continued on to the station.

The train was full but he found a seat and tucked himself behind his newspaper. When he reached London, he hailed a taxi, tipped the driver well, and asked him to deliver the envelope to Commander Scaith.

"When should it be there?" he asked.

"At this time—fifteen, maybe twenty minutes."

Kimberly saw him leave. He took the underground himself, travelling a few stations to a busy junction in the centre of London. He waited five more minutes before closing himself into a telephone box. He dialed Scaith's four-zero number. Commander Scaith answered himself.

"It's Kuzminsky," Kimberly said. "You have received my letter?"

"I have the envelope."

And the taxi driver, Kimberly thought. Scaith would have had a man waiting. The driver would have described his customer, and Kimberly had left his other coat and cap in the boot of Penny's car. Well, money was a great comfort, and Purloe's safe had provided him with more than enough to get yet another coat and hat.

"The microfilm. You find it interesting?"

"Of course I find it interesting. Kimberly was not a fool. He would not have taken rubbish."

"No. Kimberly was not a fool."

"You are now in possession of the rest of the file?"

"The rest of the microfilm has been posted to Switzerland from Woburn village. That is where it was left by Kimberly."

"I see."

The Russian was taking every precaution.

Scaith was incensed. He was enraged. Kimberly knew it.

"The exchange, money for complete file, will be made in Geneva. But I want half the money delivered to me here in England before I leave with your man for Switzerland."

"Why? Why in hell do you want to carry all that money from here to Geneva! The full amount will be paid to you in Switzerland!"

"No. That money will stay here in England for Kimberly's daughter. I will keep my word to my friend. He trusted me."

"I wouldn't trust you alone with a rubber duck! But I agree!"

"You will send your courier to children's playground at Woburn Abbey, two o'clock tomorrow afternoon. Money must be in thousand Swiss franc notes in leather case."

"Why Swiss currency if it's to be left here in England!"

"Because Swiss currency cannot be forged between now and tomorrow afternoon."

"You are a low, loathsome, cunning, viperous bastard!"

"Yes," Kimberly agreed. Your courier, he will have one pipe, sometimes smoking, sometimes in hand. He will stay ten minutes, looking at children, then walk to children's zoo. There is small shop there where children buy food for animals. He will put case on ground. I will pick it up. If money is there, I will go with your man."

"And what's to prevent us from grabbing you, taking the money and—"

"No, no. You will do nothing to me until you have all of microfilm. But if I am attacked, I have good gun. Many children could be killed. It would be very sad. And I would at once, immediately, without stop, kill myself. I have already given by post to Russia instructions for taking microfilm in Geneva if I am killed. But you send man with me to Switzerland, I see my share of money deposited in special account, and I exchange files. Remember, Commander, sir, I prefer to die now quick than return Russia and die slow or stay England and prison. Any failure from you, and Russians have the film."

"Understood. You will have no trouble leaving the country with my man or entering Switzerland. And I will always be waiting eagerly for the long, slimy arm of Russia to stretch out and grab you by your grotty throat!"

Kimberly was smiling. The old man was really steamed up.

"I will be grateful for escort. Good-bye, Commander, sir. I wish we could speak more of our friend Kimberly. Perhaps you come visit me one day, pleasant holiday."

"I will come visit you one day to put my boot up your double-dealing Russian arse!" Scaith slammed the receiver down hard, roared for Polly to summon his car. He snatched his coat, limped to the door. Polly was hovering. "Out of my way, woman! Telephone my office. I want Sir James Chorley to be there waiting for me!"

"My, we are in a tizz. Don't go falling down the steps. Have a nice day, sir."

"Be silent!"

He slipped on the first step, but his driver was there to grasp his arm and help him to the car. Polly shrugged and watched them move away.

Farquar had given Miss Clara Dredge enough time to return from her Wednesday-night special and put herself to rights. But when he arrived at number 6 Barwell Street and climbed the stairs, he found her out. Her neighbour, whom he had met the day before, offered the information that Miss Dredge had gone to the Turkish bath.

"Very clean," Farquar said.

"Oh, yes. Miss Dredge is clean. It's that damned dog!" Farquar listened while she complained about the dog, and said he would come back. "You were here yesterday. Are you a regular?" Farquar shook his head. "You'll like Miss Dredge. Someone sent you, then?" Farquar nodded his head. "I wouldn't muscle in on Miss Dredge's trade," she said. Again Farquar shook his head. " 'Specially if you're kinky and you want that bloody dog around." This time he shook his head more vehemently and found his way downstairs. The voice of Miss Dredge's neighbour floated down the stairwell. "Miss Dredge will be back by twelve. Don't let on we talked. But it's only fair to warn a new customer about that bloody dog!"

A man roasting chestnuts on the corner tried to sell him some. Farquar declined. He found a box and telephoned to Scaith. He told him Miss Dredge was out. Scaith summoned him to his office at once.

James Chorley was still there when he arrived. Scaith handed him the memo of the call from Sergei Kuzminsky. Farquar read it.

"Woburn Abbey? The man must be mad. At one o'clock the place will be overrun.

"Can you think of a better place to get lost?" Chorley scowled. "You don't appear to be on your toes today, young Farquar. Too late a night, what?"

Scaith rapped sharply on his desk.

"This is the picture: mark it Operation Grim. The Chief Constable of Buckinghamshire is co-operating: he's been onto the Duke of Bedford. His Grace is very kindly giving us an office in Woburn Abbey itself as Field H.Q. Telephone lines are being installed with a direct line to me. Sir James will leave for Woburn now. You're both booked into the Bedford Arms."

"Do I go with Sir James now?" Farquar asked.

"No. Not immediately. You follow through with the Dredge woman. If you turn up a line, set up a team to run it out. Then you follow Sir James to Woburn. We all liaise at Field H.Q. in the Abbey."

"And the money, Commander?" Chorley asked.

"Taken care of by Treasury. It will be delivered to you at the Bedford Arms in a leather case. You assign a man from your Section to be courier. If all goes to plan, we'll have our man on a plane to Geneva tomorrow night. You and Farquar will go with him to pick up the file. Your flight will be escorted by two Hunter Hawks from Air Force. If the Russkies get the slightest hint of Operation Grim, they might take the desperate shot of trying to blow you out of the sky. Understood?"

"Understood, sir."

"Get on with it."

On their way out, Scaith's secretary gave Farquar the telephone number of the Bedford Arms and the numbers of the lines being installed in Field H.Q. at Woburn Abbey. Sir James was at his most urbane.

"I daresay the Duke will ask me in to dine. I'll pop home and get packed with something formal. I'm sure you'll find dinner at the Bedford Arms is palatable."

"I enjoy a good pub meal."

Farquar saw Chorley into his car and hailed a taxi to drive him back to Barwell Street. He was terribly concerned that the chase was leading them to Woburn Abbey. The operation, as described by Scaith, sounded secure. But Farquar knew how these actions could misfire. People could lose their lives. Suppose the Russians—in fact the K.G.B.—were on to Kuzminsky and followed him to Woburn Abbey and to the children's playground? They would not hesitate to go into action. It was a nightmarish thought.

Once more he arrived at 6 Barwell Street and hurried up the stairs. He expected at least barking, if not growling, from the dog, but there was silence. He knocked gently once again and waited. Nothing. As he tiptoed away, the door across the hall creaked open. Miss Dredge's neighbour shook her head.

"She's not back. Fell onto something coming home, I expect. Now, I'm the first one to admit a dog is a good thing for getting into conversation with a trick when he's not actually on the lookout for a bit. Dredge is no fool. . . ."

"But the dog?" Farquar was curious. "Does the dog attend the Turkish bath?"

Miss Dredge's friend broke into a peal of laughter. "Who sent you? Oh, you are a card, a real card! Come in. Have a drop of gin. Dredge could be busy half the day."

She threw open the door. Farquar backed down the top step of the flight of stairs.

"So kind. But, thank you . . . no. . . ."

He turned and scurried away. The woman's wail speeded his descent.

"That bloody dog!"

But luck was with him. A woman and a dog were coming in the door.

"Miss Dredge?"

Miss Dredge eyed him.

"From the rozzers again," she stated. "Johnny Chestnut on the corner let on there was a plain-clothes fellow came here this morning and again just now."

"That's right," Farquar agreed. "He must have meant me. Could I have a word with you?"

"For all the good it will do you, you can. I told the sergeant yesterday: I don't sing to the cops." She led the way upstairs, opened her door and beckoned him in. "You'll have to pay for time," she said, looking at her watch.

"Of course, of course."

She offered him an upright chair.

"Sit down. You don't mind if I start chopping the dog's dinner?" The animal whined and moved restlessly around the room. "You'll have to wait." She put a board on the table, emptied a bag of meat, and began to chop. "All good stuff. They keep it for me in the restaurants. We have an arrangement. Not free. But all good stuff. Sometimes I'm tempted by a bit myself. But I couldn't. Really! I mean, taking from a dog!" The dog wagged his heavy tail. "Understands every word you say. Go on. Try him. You tell 'im he's a B-A-D D-O-G." She spelled it out. The dog growled, showing fangs. Miss Dredge laughed aloud. "You see? Even spells!"

Farquar's knees weakened beneath him. He bent into the upright chair.

"Yes," he said. "Very intelligent."

"Oh, if he could only talk!"

"Probably be able to take his O Levels."

161

Farquar kept a watchful eye on the animal as Miss Dredge put the board of meat on the floor. He stood up and devoured it. As soon as he had finished his meal, she hauled his heavy basket through to another room.

"Never have him in here with a customer," she said. "You know, I think he's got a jealous streak, me being his mum." She sent the dog in after his basket. "And he farts after he's been fed." She wiped the board with a bit of newspaper, put it back into a cupboard, and produced two glasses and a bottle of gin. "I like to give the police a drop. Give nothing, get nothing, I always say. Not that I am a nark." She sat down opposite to Farquar, pouring the gin. "Is he a murderer?"

"Yes. He is a murderer," he said. "He is suspected of murdering a child." This was the classic way to get information from members of the public who were unwilling to tell tales to the police.

"Jesus Christ!" Miss Dredge drank her gin, reached for the bottle to pour herself another but thought better of it. "He could have had a go at me. A girl, was it?" There was a Welsh lilt to her voice which had become more pronounced. "I wouldn't say a word if it was a smash-and-grab. The things they leave to tempt poor sods. And the insurance pays up anyway. But a little girl on 'er way home from school!" She painted the picture for herself. "The bastard asked where the buses went from. The Green Lines ones. He wanted to get the first one out to Dunstable. Pro-

162

per poorly he looked. Said he'd been in a fight. I washed the blood off his coat. I gave him breakfast. But he did pay me ten pounds to stay the night. Cried like a baby round about three o'clock. Then did the job like an eighteen-year-old and went to sleep. Might have done me in. Me *and* me dog!"

Farquar talked to her a little longer and politely drank his gin. He put two five-pound notes beside the bottle and left. He heard her talking to the dog as he closed the outer door. This time Johnny Chestnut hailed him like an old friend.

"What's up, copper?"

"Nothing's up."

"Come off it, guv. You bin up there twice."

Farquar looked him squarely in the eyes. "I'm oversexed."

In a laboratory in Clerkenwall, pictures of Kimberly taken from his new Russian passport—the Kuzminsky face staring sardonically into space—slid out of the copying machine and piled in a basket on the floor. Although none of the operators knew who he was, somehow tension grew.

"THIS MAN IS WANTED" had been scratched out. Commander Scaith had been in himself. He had done the scratching. In its place, he had scrawled: "THIS MAN MUST BE FOUND."

The woman minding the machine had been doing it since 1938. She looked down curiously at the multiple images piling up. To her, the face did not look quite real, a sort of plastic man. She knew, whoever the man was, he was for the chopper. These pictures were not for the police. This man had put himself outside the law that is guarded by the normal enforcement authorities. He was a loner with no country to fall back on. In some way, he must have betrayed the entire human race.

The cycle complete, the machine turned itself off. She gathered the pictures, made up three packages, and carried them upstairs.

Three men on motor bicycles were waiting to take them, each to a different address.

Eight

The brutal murder of Professor Purloe did not reach the newspapers until mid-morning. The early editions of the evening papers carried the details. It was agreed that robbery must have been the motive. One of the women working in his house admitted she once had seen the old man counting huge bundles of banknotes on his writing table when she had popped in to fill the flower vases with fresh water. He had been too absorbed to notice, and she had slipped out again and had never mentioned it to anyone.

No one in the household knew how to open the safe. It seemed obvious that Professor Purloe had been forced at gunpoint to work the combination himself and then been arbitrarily shot. A sad ending for such a fine old man.

The Police had called in Scotland Yard. They had found a man tied up and gagged in the summerhouse. He had been a guest of the Professor and was expected to help the police with their enquiries.

The Russians had no doubt but that Kimberly was responsible. K.G.B. agents pored over a map of the area and marked the spot with a small red flag. There were three other flags on the map, identifying the only places where it was certain Kimberly had been: one at Heathrow Airport, another pinpointing the British Foreign Office, and a third indicated plainly the area close to Putney Bridge. The man was mobile, despite the known fact that he had been wounded on the tow-path at Putney.

Another gaffe was the abduction of the wrong girl in place of Kimberly's daughter. However, the daughter herself was now being closely shadowed and, while her country cottage had been thoroughly searched, there was no trace of Kimberly having visited her. Since it was known that he had not replied to her letters since his defection, it was possible they had not been in touch. Perhaps he was trying to protect her in some quixotic Western way.

After Kimberly had finished talking with Scaith, and in spite of the final insults, he felt sure he had made a deal. He now had almost twenty-four hours in hand to prepare and plan. Having been in Special Service on the highest levels, and a double agent all his adult life, he was better equipped than most people to enter this final phase of an operation which had begun with the stealing of Purloe's files and would end with the successful selling of them and his own escape. He knew many corners of the world where he could still live in peace and greatly enjoy what years might yet be left to him.

Mountains, lakes, pastures, rock and sandy shores, sun, and snow, all were available. He could grow a few vines and pull trout out of a stream. A man who knew his way would have no trouble on a magic carpet woven of Swiss francs.

What if he became bored? He could go back into business as a mercenary. The Japanese, for instance, would give their eyes for a man of his experience and would protect him with an arsenal. The Turks and the Egyptians would come out bidding strongly to acquire him if it were known that Kimberly was not mouldering in Leningrad; in the past it had been pleasant floating on the Nile and the Bosphorus.

Kimberly walked into a new exotic male hairdressing salon.

"My boy," he said, smiling shyly, a little on the helpless side. "I badly need your advice."

He'd been foolish, had his hair dyed and styled this way, but his friends were furious. Kimberly knew well the ways and weaknesses of homosexuals. His appeal bore fruit at once.

"A wig, sir? Is that what's wanted?"

Kimberly nodded gratefully.

"A wig. Just the thing! Something fuller, perhaps. With a touch of grey. More of a father figure, hummm?"

He left with two wigs and an appointment to come back for a trim in three weeks' time. The assistants had been bowled over by his charm. They adored his false moustache. They took bets on whether he was an M.P. or a retired Major off to procure new blood.

Kimberly bought himself a travelling bag, another overcoat, and two more hats. He had them all packed into his travelling bag and took them to the men's changing room at Victoria Station.

When he emerged, he was wearing the longer grey wig beneath a Professor Higgins hat. A quietly checked sports coat covered his still-rotund figure. He carried his travelling bag and had changed his glasses yet again. He rode a taxi to the Automobile Association in Leicester Square, where he took instant passport photographs of himself in their Polaroid machine. He changed his appearance this way three times, once clean shaven and once with a padded lip. He collected the three sets of photographs, checked his bag in a left luggage office, and went to Bentley's for an excellent lunch.

All this time he was considering and discarding plans. It would be too dangerous to carry his microfilm with him under escort to Geneva. Scaith might not believe he had posted it. He might have him thoroughly searched. In Scaith's place, that was what Kimberly would do. The same search would disclose his three future identities. His three new passports would have to be sent on in advance. The travel document which Scaith would provide would obviously be worthless once their deal was done.

Kimberly paid his bill, taxied to a different area, and bought inks, pens, and a variety of metal and rubber stamps. At a locksmith's shop, he matched the impression he had taken of the church-door key at Woburn. An iron-monger sold him a metal file. He picked up shirts, ties, and underwear, a camera, a compass and field glasses, and a pair of mountain boots. A gentleman hiker and bird fancier was a welcome figure the world over and, incidentally, bird watching was a pastime he enjoyed.

If it were not for the hideous throbbing of his arm, he would have felt totally at ease. Everything was going well, and he still had plenty of time to finalise his growing plan.

Farquar ate a small lunch. He returned to his office and got his secretary to book him on the next flight to Geneva. If anyone enquired, that was the message they would get. He went home, packed a bag, and wrote a note for Penny:

Desperately sorry, love. There's a bloody personage arriving in Switzerland tonight and I must go and meet the B! Promise you I am going to change my job. Something strictly nine till five. I love you. Will bring you Easter Sunday egg and love. Farq.

He cancelled the reservation made by his secretary, carried his bag to the lift, went down, and threw it into his car. In spite of the traffic, Farquar managed successfully to exceed the speed limit on the M1 and reach Woburn in the early afternoon. He pulled up outside the Bedford Arms and carried his bag in.

His room was ready. He was glad to see he had a private bath and a telephone. He unpacked his few things, including a dinner suit.

He felt a lightness of heart as he thought of Penny and that this was the last job he would be doing for Scaith. He would be with Chorley when the transaction was concluded and stay with him, as Scaith had ordered, until the material was handed into Scaith's hand unread. That would be that. The thought of being free of Scaith inversely released a wave of affection for the lame old man. He felt impelled to telephone him and explain that, even though he was leaving the Service, he would always be there if Scaith should need a hand. He pulled himself up short. He must be mad. Offer a hand to Scaith, and he'd have your arm and get you by the throat! No! No more! He must have been mad to think of such a thing.

He rang through to the Field H.Q. Scaith had set up at Woburn Abbey. Sir James Chorley had been there, but he had gone into the park again. He would be back for tea.

"I'll come over. Where will I find you?"

"We have a man stationed at the front door. He has a key and will bring you straight up here.

Her Grace has given us two rooms, so we are comfortable."

Farquar got into his car again. How odd, indeed, to be on a spy hunt at Woburn Abbey. The old place had served its purpose during the war. This Russian bastard should have left the Bedford family in peace.

He turned left and passed the church, feeling that he ought to cross himself, if only for luck. But, as he did not believe in luck, only in being prepared, he drove on uncrossed into the park.

Although the rhododendrons blazed a magnificent welcome, and the well-kept drive lay invitingly ahead, the first lake beside the drive tempted him. He turned onto the grass, wandering on forbidden paths, refreshing his memory of the layout.

He slowed down as a keeper waved him to a stop. He explained that he was a guest at the Abbey, taking advantage of the roads closed to the public. The keeper touched his hat and had just begun to move off when a sudden *ping* left Farquar staring blindly at a completely opaque, shattered windscreen. He ducked quickly to find his gun before the next move. He inched his head up slowly, to see the keeper already standing beside him, touching the splintered screen and wagging his head knowledgeably.

" 'Tis the atmosphere," he said, quite unmoved by the damage to the car.

"But surely, you heard the shot," Farquar said patiently.

The keeper nodded agreeably. "Aye. Some of them be after squirrels today. Pretty things, but pestilential." He touched the windscreen. " 'Tis the atmosphere," he said again. "You just switch that there engine off and you'll hear it, sir." Farquar did so. "Hark, sir!" In the utter silence, he listened. A blackbird trilled mockingly and a small animal rustled in the leaves. The gamekeeper's chest wheezed, gently asthmatic, reminiscent of Scaith who had sent him on this unlikely mission. "See what I mean, sir?" Farquar nodded, waiting, wondering who else could be listening just as intently as himself, screened by the evergreens. They heard a lion roar. "The poor animals," the keeper said. "Give me the creeps. 'T'ain't natural. Kings of the jungle, that's what they are. And 'ere we 'ave 'em locked up in a bleeding park like goats . . . begging His Grace's pardon." He wheezed once more. "You better get on, sir. Get a new motorcar before 'tis dark, sir."

So much for his prized BMW, Farquar thought. Easy come, easy go. Get another one before night fell. He watched the keeper wobble away while he drove on, feeling painfully vulnerable with his head out of the side window to see where he was going.

He parked and crunched across the gravel to find the plainclothesman. It was a face he knew, one of the S.B. Section. He took Farquar inside, across the marble floor dressed with its scarlet sofas, and up two flights of stairs.

"There is a lift, sir," he said. "But, of course, we are trying to be as little trouble as possible."

"Glad to hear it."

They went into a room. A long trestle table had been set up with a typewriter and three telephones. Men's coats lay across a bed. Two men were on duty. Farquar nodded as he was led into an inner room.

"And this is where Sir James has fixed his own office."

Farquar looked around: again, a bed, this time a double one, with a bathroom leading off. He looked through the window at the view. "Very nice," he said.

"Then I'll be getting back to the front door. Matthews is the name, sir, if you should be needing me." He hesitated. "Is it true, sir, this Russian chap we're after is the fellow who cracked our copper's skull up Putney way?"

Farquar gave him a surprised look.

"Rumours, Matthews. Anyway, I'm always the last to know."

Matthews smirked. He knew better. He knew Farquar was one of their top young chaps.

"Sorry, sir. Should never have asked."

Farquar opened his dispatch case and pulled out a dozen enlarged copies of the Kuzminsky passport photograph.

"Photos of the subject," he said. "For Section use only. Not to be passed on to the local police or C.I.D. until we have further orders. Understood?"

"Understood, sir."

"Thank you, Matthews."

"Thank you, sir."

Matthews left with the photographs. Farquar picked up the internal phone and asked to be connected to Her Grace. He gave his name. The Duchess was ecstatic in her welcome. "But you must come down at once to the drawing room and have tea."

"I'm here on duty."

"That is just nonsense. You come down or I will come and bring you here. Your mad friend Chorley has been out shooting. Rabbits, he says. I don't think he can tell a rabbit from one of my lovely wallabies. I am terribly worried for my lovely wallabies. Come down at once!"

Farquar paused in the other room.

"Anything moving?"

"One Green Line driver says he thinks he saw our man. But as he was driving to Kent and our Miss Dredge said the Russkie spoke of going north, it doesn't seem to tally."

"Never know. Maybe he was leading our Miss Dredge astray."

"Likely, sir. But we're going through the lot."

"Keep at it," Farquar said. "And, by the way: someone took a shot at me in the park. At the car, anyway, so I might assume it was at me. Shattered the windscreen. Can't believe it's anything to do with the job here. Maybe someone just doesn't like me or hates German cars. Anyway, put a man onto it, and I'll need another car. Have one sent out from the pool."

One man got to his feet. "Might have killed you, sir. The same man that bashed the Putney cop."

So much for security, Farquar thought bitterly. In fact, he could well have been killed but, in this most discreet of all Special Services, how was it common knowledge that the Russian Kuzminsky had fought the policeman on the towpath? Christ, were there leaks? Scaith was right. Someone was for the high-jump—and none too soon.

"Now hear this," Farquar said, his voice clipped. "The man we want is a Russian defector. He has information for sale. We want that information." Now he was copying Scaith. "The man who tangled with our hero on the towpath was probably I.R.A. He is possibly chucking a bomb somewhere in a Chelsea pub right now. That's all there is to it. Understood?"

"Understood, sir."

"Then keep your facts in order!"

"Yes, sir."

"I'll be down in the drawing room with Her Grace." Farquar took the lift downstairs. He put his arms round the Duchess, kissed her. "My, my," he murmured. "How nice to again embrace Miss Nicole Nobody!"

"Ah, you have read my book, yes?"

"More than once . . . certain passages."

"Then you will be interested in what I did *not* write! I will tell you everything. You are coming for dinner tonight." It was a command. "I have also invited your funny friend."

"Sir James? You've said that twice. What's so funny about him?"

"Funny-peculiar, as you say. Dinner will be very dull. All the exciting guests are coming to-morrow night. Why haven't we heard from you? You could have come for the week-end. How long will your officers be keeping one of my best rooms?" She rattled on, asking questions and answering them herself. "I know. Until you catch these drug-pushers. Pushers near Woburn? Mostly it is just *climbers!* But you have been in America. Did you like it? We were in Australia and Japan. I must tell you all about Japan. Sit down. Have your tea. Wait until I tell you everything."

She crossed to a side table to pour tea. The Duke came in. Farquar and he shook hands.

"Do you mind?" said the Duke, smiling as he nursed his fingers. "Writer's cramp. I've signed God knows how many autographs since lunch. No wonder I loathe signing cheques!" The Duchess brought them tea as the Duke continued: "We get all the news. My butler just heard from one of your men that the man who attacked the policeman was a member of the I.R.A. Not a dope peddler at all. So what are you doing here?"

"Oh, he does a little pushing on the side."

Farquar could have flung his cup into the fire-place with rage.

"And I've heard about the lunatic from the asylum who tried to murder you."

"Murder Farq?" The Dutchess clutched his arm. "I know that a lunatic had—"

The Duchess broke off. Everyone was looking at James Chorley. He had come in from the library, dressed in tweed knickerbockers and highly polished leather gaiters.

"Fourteen squirrels," he said breezily and clamped his arm around Farquar's shoulder. "How are you, old man? Not suffering from shock?"

"No. My windscreen shattered. Happens all the time."

The Duchess said her windscreen had shattered once. Chorley released Farquar from his embrace. His face shining with health, he turned to Her Grace.

"And you must tell me all about it." He pushed a bloody bunch of squirrel tails towards Farquar. "Here. You have these. Pity you missed the sport."

Retreating, Farquar held up his hands.

"Thank you, no, Sir James. To the hunter his spoils."

He excused himself. His mind was spinning. What was this idiocy? What had Scaith been thinking, dropping him unwarned into a mad drawing-room farce?

He went upstairs again and asked to be driven to the Bedford Arms. At the hotel, he flung himself disgusted onto his bed. He would have liked to talk to Penny, but he had told her he would be in Switzerland. However, Saturday would see the matter closed.

He shut his eyes.

Penny worked hard throughout the day. She had shopped for dinner during the lunch hour and had spent her tea break alone, scanning the papers. The headlines told of a murdered professor. Inside there was a piece about Kimberly's funeral in Leningrad. The British Consul had attended, but not in his official capacity. He had declined to comment on whether or not he had been a personal friend of Kimberly. Penny tried to remember. Had he had many friends? It didn't seem so. Looking back, they had spent a lot of time alone together. The jolly father and the growing child. One day she would tell Farquar all about it, the whole tale. He might not believe her.

She left the Dorchester at half-past five, several invitations for dinner politely refused. Farquar would be waiting. She longed to change her clothes, but decided she would get Farquar to take her to her flat, just in case some clever journalist was still pursuing her. With the Kimberly funeral in the news, there was still that chance.

She wondered where she and Farquar would live eventually. Would his flat be big enough? Well, to start with, anyway. There was her cottage. But even that, somehow, would never be the same again; that chalked circle with the "P" in the centre, the tail of the "P" pointing to her garden shed, and Philip hiding: a dream she had indulged in for so long and which, in the end, turned out to be a nightmare. Poor Philip. She had had to help him. What else could she have done? And yet, strangely, somehow the whole episode had brought her closer to Farq, clarified her feelings about him so that, with the nightmare over and waking up, they had become engaged.

Penny let herself into Farquar's flat. She went straight into the kitchen with her carrier bag, unpacked it and prepared the ice bucket for drinks. She took it into the sitting room and poured herself a gin and tonic before she saw his note. Her whole being cried out No! it could not be true. She had been keyed up to meet him, to play housewife in contrast to the evening out the night before.

She sipped her drink sadly, suddenly realising she was very tired. Looking back, she had not let up since Tuesday, two days ago. And what did Farq's note say? She checked it:

I love you. Will bring you Easter Sunday egg.

That left only Friday and Saturday. Her practical nature got to work. She decided to have a light supper, go to bed and sleep, and be up long before any eager journalist would be at large. She would go to her own flat, quickly grab her clothes, and come back to install herself in a tiny corner of Farq's flat. She had already decided on which cupboard would be hers.

She would have to work on Friday morning but would fill the afternoon by rearranging what would now be their mutual flat. The evening . . . evenings had never been a problem to her as a single girl. But, since yesterday, she was a single girl no more. In her new, ecstatic state, any evening without Farq loomed empty. She would go to the cinema. The next day would be pushed along by shopping for fresh food. She would take a sauna bath, have her hair and toes and nails made perfect, sleep early again, waiting for her Easter egg. That was it.

She began to put her program into practice immediately. She finished her drink and ran a bath, looking forward to a supper of ham and eggs, supplemented by the telly. She floated in her bath, planning what she would get married in.

Kimberly returned by train, picked up Penny's car, and drove to the place he had used to change in before setting out. He arrived back at the Bull Hotel in the same clothes he had worn when Penny brought him there. He carried his bag upstairs and ordered a tray of tea.

He went to work on the three passports he had taken from Purloe's house. It was fiddling work, but he was good at it. During his active career, he had had to do without the experts from time to time, and he had acquired a variety of skills. It was a better start than he had had once before when a crisis had driven him underground. That time he had found his way from Istanbul to Dublin with homemade papers. By comparison, his present task was child's play.

He had the passports finished before the local post closed down for the night. He went out to express them in three registered envelopes, addressed to himself at three different towns in Switzerland.

Back at the Bull, he bought Douglas and Pauline an early drink. He thanked them again for their kindness and went back to his room, promising to come down later for a bite.

Now the time had come to remove the bandage Penny had put on his upper arm. The wound was festering. He cleaned it with antiseptic and bound it with a towel torn in strips. The pills Penny had provided might have cleared up a tooth abscess but, as for his bullet wound, they did not apppear to be taking effect. He knew it could be serious. The best thing he could do was rest as much as possible and then demand immediate medical help as soon as he was with Scaith's contact the following day. A massive shot of penicillin should clear up the infection before it spread. The last thing Scaith would want was a delirious incompetent on his hands when he needed immediate action.

Kimberly took out his metal file and selected from his assortment of keys. With the same meticulous patience he had used to prepare the passports, he began to file. He might never need the key, but he would not be unprepared.

His present plan was to go to Switzerland, secure in the company of Special Branch men, plead ill health because of the bullet wound, and rest. He would be thoroughly protected for at least a night. The following day, when he was sure the full sum of money had been deposited in the numbered account, he would explain he had left the microfilm in England. Naturally, Special Branch would stay close to him in Geneva until it was in Scaith's hands. After that, he would be of little interest to the British. Special Branch would not want to be involved in a killing so far away from their own turf. He would not be worth the risk. They would let him go.

He completed two keys to his own satisfaction and, although his arm and head were throbbing, he went down to the dining room. He would have to hold himself together for a short while longer, and that was that. Nothing he had not done before. He kept repeating it to himself.

Nine

Farquar was disturbed by knocking on his door. He stood up and smoothed his hair.

"Come in."

It was Matthews, the man on the door at Woburn.

"Sorry, sir, but I was going off duty when the news came in. So, being on the leg, as it were, I came to tell you. Save you going over there."

"What's going on?" Farquar perched himself on the side of the bed. "Don't tell me they got him?"

"Oh, no, sir. But they found a woman. She's certain. Sure she's seen him. She isn't in any doubt."

"And they're the worst."

Matthews laughed. "Well, she's got a sick sister near Dunstable. On Wednesday she wakes early, very early. Says she felt uneasy about this sister. So she ups and takes the first bus leaving on that route."

"Green Line?"

"Right, sir. We've got several fellows at that bus stop flashing the Russian's picture to the long-distance passengers. Well, this afternoon, going out to visit the sister again, she takes one look at the face and says, 'Yes—I've seen that man.'"

"She was sure of the day?"

"No question."

"What made her so definite it was the same face?"

Matthews guffawed again. "Said she fancied him. Told our man not to be cheeky when he asked her did she fancy many fellows. Said she was not that kind."

"So she thought this one something special."

"That's right, sir. Well, our man gave her a cup of tea and then went on the bus with her because she wasn't sure where the Russian got off."

"Did she *say* the chap was Russian?"

"No, sir. That never entered into it. And our man never suggested it."

"She didn't hear him speak?"

"Yes, sir. And that's the puzzling part. Said they passed a few civil words, as travellers do, and she was sure he was a—a—"

"Toff" Farquar suggested.

"That's the word, sir. Yes."

"And did she remember where this attractive toff got off the bus?"

"Well, she got off at Dunstable and she knows he got off before. She's not sure if it was one or two stops. Said she must've dozed, being an early bus."

"Sir James has had all this?"

"Yes, sir. Came straight through on our field lines. Three memo-copies typed up. I got a look at one, Sir James has his. Other's on Section file."

Farquar thought for a moment before speaking.

"And you didn't come to report on Sir James's orders?"

"No, sir. As I said, I came on my own. On my way for a pint, sir."

Again Farquar hesitated, a thin frown now racing across his face. He stood up.

"Most kind of you, Matthews. I suppose we're covering the area where our lady said the man might have left the bus."

"Working till shuteye, sir: pubs, cinemas, anywhere people can be found we'll have a man. And up with the milk van in the morning. We'll have him, sir. You get a good night's sleep."

Farquar was interested to know what part Matthews would play in this activity. He sounded so involved.

"And you?" he asked.

"I'm going to a bingo hall with a young lady I met over at the big house."

When Matthews left, Farquar rang through to Field H.Q. at Woburn. Everything Matthews had reported was true. But Sir James had left. Farquar telephoned to Commander Scaith. He, too, had already had the news.

"Spreading the net, old man." Scaith sounded in good spirits. "We'll pull him in."

"I'm sure. But I find it hard to see my particular function here. You briefed us, but Sir James has given me no instructions since our meeting with you. In fact, he hasn't really spoken to me except to crash a very private dinner I was having with Miss Kimberly when we became engaged."

"You've seen him at Woburn, haven't you?"

"Only to be offered some bloody squirrel tails!"

"Squirrel tails?" Scaith rasped. "What's bloody squirrel tails got to do with all this!"

"Only God and Sir James can answer that. And neither one seems to be paying me much attention at the moment. Why did he ask for me? What's he waiting for?"

"Probably waiting for the action to get rough." Scaith cleared his throat. "Matter of fact, been wondering what he's up to myself. Never mentions you. Even though it was you, of course, who got us off the ground with Miss Dredge. Very uncommunicative before. What did you do to her, eh? Tickle her fancy?"

Scaith roared with laughter. Farquar waited patiently for it to stop.

"And I'm to stay on here with Sir James?"

"He's setting up another field office. Back of a pub at Maidenhead. The Green Man. Our Kuzminsky went in that direction. We have the date with him tomorrow afternoon at Woburn. Somewhere between the two places we may come on him unawares."

"I'll be there at first call tomorrow."

"I saw the signal that you had trouble with your car. You'll find one of our Jaguars outside the Bedford Arms."

"Thank you, sir."

"And you're to bring me the Kimberly files, unread, remember!"

Farquar sighed. "From Kuzminsky the UnRed. You can be assured of that, sir."

"Oh, I am, I am. Enjoy your Easter!"

Scaith hung up abruptly. Farquar decided to bathe and shave. Something had to be washed off. He soaked himself, and by working the taps with his toes, he was able to keep the water at a steady temperature for almost half an hour. Then playtime started running out.

He had climbed from his bath and shaved, a towel tied round his waist, when he sensed he was no longer alone. His only weapon was the cutthroat razor. He grasped it firmly and peered into the steamed-up mirror. He saw the man behind him. He braced himself. The intruder raised his hands shoulder-high, palms exposed, innocently naked.

It was James Chorley, but Farquar hardly recognised him. This was not the dapper Sir James of the Mirabelle who had flirted with Penelope, nor the country-clad squire from the drawing-room, brandishing his squirrel tails.

This man was sinister. He wore a soft silk robe as though it were an extra skin. It slid across his massive frame obscenely, exposing what it should have concealed, and he was bald. This Chorley was as bald as a billiard ball.

In the mirror, Chorley saw Farquar's eyes fasten on his domed skull.

"Like a prick," Chorley said. "Don't you think it's like a prick?" He admired himself in the full-length mirror on the bathroom door, pulling his robe aside. He considered the reflection of his private parts. "Maybe not like Mr. Mouse . . . but like a big, aggressive prick." He turned back to Farquar. "You think me vulgar, don't you?" Farquar did not answer him. "Paul Ives liked my vulgarity. He liked my . . . actually, very few people know I wear a wig. Don't think even old Scaith knows. I have four wigs, all sitting on their stands, all different lengths. I change them every week, in rotation. And then, when it looks as though I need a trim, I return to number one."

"Which number do you wear for squirrel shooting?" Farquar asked dryly.

He dropped his razor into the wash-basin and turned off the taps. Chorley shook his head, leaned past him and turned both the hot and cold water on again. He went to the bath and began running the water there.

"Walls are thin," he whispered. He tapped the wall. "Really only a partition."

"So what?"

Farquar pulled a dressing gown over his damp

body. He was furious, uncomfortable, and clammy. He turned towards the bedroom, but Chorley, peculiarly light on his feet, whipped in front of him.

"Much better in here with the taps on. Don't be an ass."

Farquar looked at him coldly. "I've begun to feel like an ass."

Chorley pointed at the cork-topped stool, inviting him to sit, choosing the lavatory seat for himself. Farquar remained aggressively upright. It was his bathroom and Chorley was uninvited. But Chorley was complaisant, shrugging. "Never stand if you can sit," he advised.

Chorley leant back, making himself as comfortable as possible. Farquar stared with loathing at the big bull-neck he had never before seen without a tie. The shoulders bulged under the silk robe. The forearms emerged huge and hairy. Chorley presented a complete contrast to the façade he usually displayed. Yet, under scrutiny, he remained utterly at ease. He loosened the robe about his neck, exposing an equally hirsute chest which he then scratched with evident pleasure.

Farquar's antipathy increased. He resented the invasion of his bathroom. He found it offensive, particularly when he recalled Penny's laughter in the night. Chorley had told her that Paul Ives and he had had a homosexual relationship. Suddenly Farquar dropped the official status supposed to be in existence between himself and Sir

James. He turned on him with tight anger. "What is this, Chorley? What do you want with me?"

"Dear boy, dear boy." Chorley raised his palms and his eyebrows. "Only a little friendly conversation. You were the last one to be with Paul. I had an affection for dear Paul. And I thought you might tell me of his . . ." Chorley broke off, peering intently into Farquar's face. "But I see it's a sensitive subject. For you as well as for me."

"A melancholy subject. And, as far as I am concerned, closed."

"As you wish, my dear fellow." Chorley sighed deeply. "As you wish . . ."

"And it seems to me that I might just as well have gone to Scotland on holiday as kicking my heels here."

"Snorting to get into battle, eh?" Chorley made one of his lightning moves. He leant forward and caught Farquar's dressing-gown cord. "But you have been in the firing-line already once today? Tell me about the accident to your car. Did you see anyone?" he asked gently, holding onto the cord.

The knot came undone. Farquar snatched it back from Chorley's hand and retied it impatiently.

"A stray bullet," he said curtly.

"Ah, yes. A stray bullet. Some idiot playing with guns. We can always count on some idiot playing with guns."

Chorley laughed silently, the fleshy layer shaking over his bulging muscles. He reached for the cord again, but Farquar stepped back smartly, frustrating him.

"Nobody else will get a hot bath if we use all the water," he said angrily.

Chorley nodded amiably. He got to his feet to turn off the hot taps.

"Cold will probably do," he whispered. "What did you think of old Scaith's office?" He didn't wait for an answer. "All done up, all those buttons, jukebox and liqueurs? What's he up to?" Again he went on without pause. "Barmy, if you ask me. Take this business. He could have held Kuzminsky and roasted the goods out of him. He had the chance."

Farquar jumped to the defence of Scaith. "An old man crippled fighting for his country? Faced by a man who could stun a young constable with a single blow?"

"Really! Really, Farquar! You are speaking like a pompous ass! But then, you've always been the 'Mander's boy, haven't you? Sooner or later, someone will have to take his place. Don't you find yourself a little youthful for the role?"

"I'm leaving the Service immediately after the Kimberly file has been turned over to Scaith."

Chorley's eyebrows shot up.

"Well! You are, are you? Interesting." He sighed deeply. "How strange."

"Nothing strange about it."

"I was thinking of that Great Chess Player in the sky. If you had resigned the game just before your last assignment in America, Paul Ives might still be alive and well and living in London."

Farquar decided to let it ride. He gestured to the door. "If you'll excuse me now, Sir James, I'll finish getting dressed."

He went into the bedroom. Light-footed, Chorley followed behind him. He held Farquar's cutthroat razor in his hand. Farquar turned to face him. Chorley held the razor up.

"Safety razor is the thing, old boy. These are dangerous toys.'

"They do the job."

Chorley nodded grave agreement and in the doorway he handed the razor to Farquar. Suddenly he was all smiles, a guest leaving after a pleasant chat and a brimming glass.

"That's me over there." He pointed to a room across the corridor. "Nice and close. What a curious life it is. I'll see you at dinner, then. I had no idea you were such a friend of the Duke."

"We know each other."

"And where is Miss Kimberly tonight?"

"With friends."

"How very nice. And the wedding?"

"Fairly soon."

"You will ask me, of course?"

"It will be a quiet wedding."

"And so it should be! Well, on with the motley." Chorley crossed the corridor to his own door. "And you won't let on about my wigs, will you?"

Chorley smiled conspiratorially and went into his room.

Farquar had toyed his way through a soufflé of artichoke at the Château de Madrid, looking bird's-eye at the magic coastline from Monte Carlo, past St. Jean Cap Ferrat to Nice and away to a twinkling beyond. He had munched contentedly in his favourite bistros everywhere: eaten, he could truthfully say, from one end of the world and back. Yet, there was something about dinner at Woburn Abbey, a certain air of carnival underlying the grandeur which invariably turned the evening into a festival as well as a feast. Furthermore, he was fond of Canelettos, and it gave him the greatest pleasure to see twenty-one of them decorating the dining room walls in a private house. He stuck his neck out to preserve democracy: he believed in a privileged class. He fought to maintain it. The war was always today.

That evening, the small party floated in to dinner on a wave of champagne. Candles and blazing logs brought the gilded side-tables and burnished urns to glittering life. Light danced among the branches of an exquisite chandelier, and the table itself drew a sigh of pleasure from the guests as each found his place.

Footmen began to pour wine, and the clear reds of the room penetrated insidiously. Everybody looked warm and expectant. The Duke sat opposite the Duchess in the centre of the table, rather than one of them at either end. In spite of the presence of the Chief Constable and his wife, no one mentioned the missing man. It appeared to be a purely social evening with each one enjoying the room and the food and the wine.

After coffee and liqueurs, a footman announced candlelight was ready for Her Grace. The candlelight tour of Woburn was something for even the blasé to enjoy. Here was Woburn as it had been some hundreds of years ago. Time slipped away to music by Boccherini and by Gluck.

All through the famous house they wandered, the Duchess chatting and explaining to those ahead, and the Duke bringing up the rear, telling lesser-known and sometimes ribald tales about his ancestors.

Farquar fell back a step or two, letting the sense of timelessness envelop him. At last, they reached the Duke's Corridor. There they were, thirteen Dukes of Bedford in an upper house of their own, a silent Parliament: twelve before John, the thirteenth Duke, who was Ian, his friend. He paused by Hastings, the ninth Duke, to study him more closely. He stopped again by another Hastings, who had been the twelfth, and caught up with the others only as they started to discuss the portrait of the present Duke.

The family likeness among these three was uncanny. The two Hastings and Ian Bedford could be the same man. Farquar felt impelled to take Ian's arm, to feel him, his flesh and bone, for the others were dead and this one, too, could die if some maniac, a self-indulgent criminal, started shooting within the walls. How dared Kuzminsky choose Woburn for his crooked dealing!

The Duke turned to Farquar and smiled. He stared somewhat ruefully at his ancestors. "It's a bit much," he said.

Farquar, however, detected the pride he took in his heritage. The Duke turned away to his other guests. Farquar watched him going. It was only then that he committed himself finally. He would see Kuzminsky dead, if necessary, to protect his friends.

Ten

Penny woke early on Good Friday morning. The bedclothes had slipped to the floor. She was alone and cold. She rearranged the blankets, trying to gather warmth and sleep again, but without success. It was no good. She might as well get dressed and do as she had planned: go early to her flat and pack some things. She saw it was not quite seven. She made a cup of tea, and put on her same grey flannel dress again, feeling as though she had worn it for a year. She called a taxi from the rank and went down the road to wait for it.

There were already some early travellers on the road. A few doors up, a man was polishing his car. A van she had seen the day before was stationary across the road with a driver at the wheel. A taxi arrived. She gave her own address. What a lot had happened since she had left there a few days ago. She found her keys as the lift carried her upstairs.

The light was on in the small entrance hall. The maid, Penny thought. The L-shaped room was spotless, exactly as it had been except for flowers which had died and her girlfriend Susan's bag. Susan had only one bag, and it was famous. She boasted that she could manage for a month if she had her bag. Now it was spilling on the table beside the telephone.

A quick look round told Penny there was no one in the kitchen or the bedroom. She knocked on the bathroom door and called Susan's name. The bathroom was empty, too. Sudden terror mounted in Penny, drying her mouth with fear. Kimberly had warned her. Susan's address book lay beside the handbag near the telephone. She must call Susan's boyfriend. Perhaps he could explain.

Ginger . . . Ginger . . . what was his name? Masters. Yes, Ginger Masters. She looked under the M's. There was no Masters. She flicked through Susan's book to G. There it was: just Ginger. Penny dialled. After a long time, someone answered her.

"Hello? Who do you want?"

"Ginger Masters, please."

"Ginger! Christ! He's way upstairs. He'll be asleep."

"It's terribly important. It's really serious. Please."

"Sue? Hey, is that you, Sue, you bitch?"

"No. I'm—I don't know where Susan is. I'm

sorry to have disturbed you but I must speak to Ginger now."

"Okay. Hold on. Bloody cold down in this hall without any socks. Hold on."

Penny waited. At last, she heard the sound of arguing voices and footsteps coming closer to the telephone.

"Hello?"

"Oh, Ginger! It's Penny. Thank goodness I got you. Where is Sue?"

"How in hell do I know where she is?" Ginger's voice was heavy with resentment. "I don't give an F where she is! I haven't heard from her."

Penny was busy rifling through Susan's bag. She found her own door key.

"But her bag is here, Ginger. Lying open in my flat. She's been here. . . ."

"Been there with some other chap. I've had it!"

"Oh, no, Ginger. That's not true, I know it's not. Listen, Ginger, listen: I know you'll think I'm mad but please believe me. I'm afraid she—she might have been kidnapped."

"What?"

"Kidnapped, Ginger!"

"Sounds as though you keep saying 'kidnapped.' "

"Yes, yes!"

"Balls!"

"Ginger. You know me. I don't play nasty jokes, and I'm not a hysteric. Something has happened to Sue. My God, Ginger, you know how hard she has to work at it to get away to be with you. She must have had the chance too late to phone me. Please, Ginger, please! You must come here at once!"

There was a silence. And, finally, her alarm seemed to reach him. He dropped his aggressive tone and spoke quietly. "You really think something has happened to Susan?"

"Something very serious. Take a taxi. Tell the driver to blow the horn. I'll come down and pay. I know you haven't any money to spare and—"

"I'll be there."

She heard him hang up and she again went through Susan's bag. Even her purse of small change was there and a carefully folded pound note. Susan would not have gone out even to buy a newspaper without her money purse or the keys to the flat. Penny looked at her watch. It was going on eight. She called the Bull Hotel. Douglas answered. She tried, without success, to keep the strain from her voice.

"Doug? It's Penny. Something has come up and I must speak to Farq—to Harold Farquar. I know it's early but please call him."

"What's up, Penny? You sound—"

"No, no. Nothing serious."

"Hold on, girl."

Philip Kimberly was running a fever. His fingers were swelling and a sharp, jagged pain kept shooting through his head. He had managed to fall into an uneasy doze when the telephone rang. He reached for it.

At the reception desk, Douglas was worried

about Penny. Although it was strictly against the hotel rules and his own ethic, he held one button down and heard Kimberly's voice.

"Hello? Yes?"

"Phil. It's me. Penny."

She had told Douglas and Pauline the man's name was Harold. Why did she call him Phil? Douglas clamped the receiver close to his ear.

"Yes, Penny?"

"A girl came unexpectedly and let herself into my flat yesterday. Susan Peters. And she's gone."

"Susan? Who is—I don't understand you."

"A girl who came to my flat. I just arrived. And she's not here."

"Probably gone home."

"No. She's left her bag. I'm afraid they've taken her. Mistook her for me. I must call the police. I must tell them about—"

"No! Don't do that!" He raised his voice harshly. "Don't you dare do that! She'll come to no harm. You must give me till tonight!"

"She could be dead by then!"

"Nonsense! She's no good to them dead! They'll try to get word to me somehow. Besides, the girl's got a tongue, hasn't she? She can explain!"

"In Russian?"

"You're being hysterical!"

"I know I am!"

"You must calm down. I promise you, no real harm will come to her. I'll speak to the Soviet Embassy myself."

"I don't believe you, Phil."

"There is nothing more I can do now."

"Yes. There is. You must come to London immediately. We'll go to the Soviet Embassy together."

Kimberly's head was cracking open. His arm felt like a blazing log.

"I can't! Don't you understand? I can't do—" He broke off, sudden fear gripping his throat. "Penny—where are you speaking from?"

"My flat. Where Susan—" Kimberly hung up abruptly. Penny heard the line go dead. "Hello, hello?" she said, although she knew she had been cut off deliberately. She hung up slowly.

Douglas Ransom's instinct was to go straight upstairs and tackle the man he knew as Harold Farquar, the man whom Penny had called Phil, but he heard his wife and went into the kitchen. Pauline was dressed in slacks, ready to go out.

"I'm late," she said. "Got to get the flowers."

"Pauline. That man upstairs. He's been on the blower, shouting at Penny."

"Been listening in, have you!"

"No. Really, Pauline. I think this is something bad." She went to the back door. Douglas followed after her. "Something about a missing girl and Russians and—"

"Russians!" she snorted. "Have a cup of tea. When the lorry comes from Covent Garden, you have to be there or you get the dregs. I'll be back in fifteen minutes. You can tell me all about it then. Russians!"

Douglas was accustomed to being bossed by

Pauline. He poured himself a cup of tea automatically, and went with it to the front bar. He began his morning routine of checking out the bottles. There were four empties. He rolled back the rug covering the cellar door and lifted up the flap. He was beginning to believe he had never listened to the telephone conversation: yet, he looked thoughtfully up the stairs before negotiating the steps into his cellar.

When Kimberly had hung up on Penny, he staggered to the wash basin and splashed his face under the running tap. He swallowed two more pain killers. From the window, he saw Pauline get into the van and drive away. Now was the time to go. Now. Decision cleared his head. He dressed quickly, packed his bag and went downstairs. He saw Douglas at the bar, adjusting the fresh bottles in their rack.

"Ah, there you are. I was about to look for you. Penny telephoned. I'm off to pick her up." He smiled gently, one mature man in rapport with another. "You know what young girls are. Easter frolic." He put his bag down and found his new wallet. "I think there are some extras to pay."

"Now you look here!" Douglas stepped out from behind his bar. "I heard you speaking to that girl. You are not going to leave my hotel until you have explained yourself."

"What on earth—"

"I think I will leave this to the police."

Douglas stretched out his hand towards the telephone extension, but Kimberly was before him. He scooped up the instrument and hit Douglas very hard with it. Half-stunned, Douglas still tried to come back at him but, tripped by the rug, he pitched down the cellar steps. He cried out once before the thud as he hit the stone floor. Then there was silence.

Kimberly stepped forward and stared down the cellar steps. Douglas lay sprawling awkwardly. Kimberly waited for him to move but Douglas did not move. Kimberly went down to him. He found his neck was broken. Moving like an automaton, Kimberly rolled the body to a corner and covered it with crates and sacks. He went back up the ladder, closed the hatch, wiped the scuff marks away and unrolled the rug. He dusted himself down. Replacing the telephone which was beginning an impatient buzz, he left.

Commander Scaith was breakfasting when Polly brought him in a letter delivered by hand. The man was waiting.

"A gentleman," she explained. "A very nice gentleman with a moustache."

Scaith slit the envelope open with his breadknife and withdrew the note. It was from the fingerprint section at Scotland Yard, signed by Cameron. Cameron said he had news of such importance for the Commander that he did not feel it was right to speak of it on the telephone.

"Where is the messenger?" Scaith asked.

"He seemed such a nice gentleman, I took him

in the kitchen. Didn't seem right to leave him kicking in the hall."

"Kicking?"

" 'Anging around. Standing when he could sit down."

"Bring him in here. And, as he's such a nice gentleman, you may fetch another cup."

Cameron was duly seated in front of Scaith, across the table with a cup of tea. Polly stood around. Scaith glared at her. Polly did her usual flounce, took up an unused ashtray and an empty wastepaper basket before she left.

Cameron unzipped a leather envelope. He offered Scaith an enlarged set of fingerprints.

"These are the prints taken from the armchair at the F.O. Mr. Milroy's office."

Scaith looked at them.

"And—?"

"And . . ." Cameron waited his moment. He drew out another set of prints which he did not immediately offer. "I came in seven o'clock this morning, knowing it was urgent, as I was off to my wee daughter for the week-end. She is married now."

"Indeed."

Scaith held out his hand.

"The matching prints," Cameron said, but still hugged them. "You will see, sir, why I felt it the best—the only thing to do—when I decided to come straight to you."

Cameron put his second set of prints into

Scaith's hand. Scaith looked at them and dropped his eyes to the caption on the bottom.

"Good God!" he whispered.

"Aye."

"Kimberly?"

"Aye."

"Kimberly!"

"Aye."

"You are saying these two sets of prints are the prints of the same man?"

"Aye."

For a long, long moment, Scaith stared down at the prints in heavy silence.

"I cannot believe it," Scaith whispered.

"Aye. Hard to believe, sir." Cameron picked up the two sets of prints. "But seeing is believing."

"But I saw something else, Cameron," Scaith snapped. "I saw the man who left these prints!"

"Ah? Kimberly?"

"It was *not* Kimberly! I knew him like a—a brother! And there was no resemblance—none whatsoever!—between the man I talked to and Philip Kimberly!" He poked angrily at the evidence. "This—*your* Kimberly—years younger, for a start!"

"I canna help that, sir," Cameron said stubbornly. "The prints canna lie. And the prints canna be loaned by one man to another to use for a week-end. Only in science fiction, sir."

"And we are not living in the world of Professor Fred Hoyle, Cameron!"

"Aye. The point, sir: a print canna lie . . . but a man's face can." Cameron's eyes lit up. "Transformation. Ladies do it, so I've been told, as well as criminals trying to create a new identity."

Scaith stared at Cameron in silence, eyes almost opaque.

"Transformation," he whispered. "New identity." He thumped the table. "Bless you, Cameron! Eureka! The transformation. Yes! The print does *not* lie! Only the face: They *did* transform him. They brought him here for a purpose which only *he* could accomplish for them. Yes!"

"Why, then, did they not burn his fingerprints with acid? They can be destroyed."

"Because, Cameron, they—oh, the arrogant fools! the contemptuous, over-confident blunderers!—they had no intention of letting their man out of their clutch until he had served his purpose. And then—the chop! He wasn't going to put his fingers on anything except the—" Suddenly Scaith began to laugh. It was an ugly laugh. He had been made a fool of. He did not enjoy being made a fool of. "The trickster," he gasped through his laughter. "The dear, lovely, talented trickster! Not finished with his trickery yet!"

"Rabbie Burns said it, sir," Cameron said reverently. "Oh, what a tangled web we weave . . ."

Scaith dried his eyes with his napkin and blew his nose volcanically. "And no one knows of these prints? No machine minder, no file clerk, no charwoman, no one at all?"

"Only the two of us."

"And that is the way it must remain." Scaith stood up, went to his desk and unlocked a drawer. "I'll keep the prints here."

"With respect, sir. I am sorry, but they must be returned to my files. We have only the one set of Philip Kimberly."

"You *had* only one set!"

"Again, with respect, sir," Cameron repeated stubbornly. "I must replace them. They will be more than safe with me."

Scaith considered the dour Scottish face. He knew when to submit gracefully and make it seem a victory.

"All things considered, Cameron, I want you to keep these prints in your safe custody. You have done splendidly. You have thrown light into darkness. Thank you, Cameron. You will be mentioned in Birthday Honours, a few letters after your name. Something to be proud of."

Cameron dropped his eyes and blushed. "The wee gurl would be that pleased," he said.

Scaith himself escorted Cameron to the door, watching as he folded his length into a Mini Minor. He stalled his engine twice, jerking to a halt before he got away. He was obviously overcome.

Back at his breakfast table, Scaith allowed himself a few minutes of reverie and an extra slice of toast and marmalade before he made contact with the new Field H.Q. at The Green Man in Maidenhead.

Cameron's great news he hugged to himself

like a hot water bottle inside his coat. Kimberly alive. Kimberly back in the game. All the flavour which he had lately missed in life came flooding back. He tasted it.

He called Polly to bring him a fresh pot of tea.

Kuzminsky had never existed. Kimberly. How splendidly Kimberly had disposed of that policeman, less than half his age. That had been done with style. Not one cry in the dark as he fell. Of course, the woman who heard Kimberly call out knew him for a toff. Of course she did! The very way he had handled his arrival at the airport had style. Pinching Milroy's coat, walking out cool as a cucumber, smacked of Kimberly. God, Polly made good marmalade. No wonder he had never settled for a wife. Kimberly's wife Annabelle was the only one he could have allowed himself to love. And now Farquar was about to marry Kimberly's daughter. It all tied up. But how?

How would Farquar react to this astounding news? Scaith knew exactly how he would react. He would protect her with every means he had. Would Farquar do as Scaith had done: allowing Annabelle Kimberly to feel she had crept out unknown to Switzerland when all the while she had been the bait? He had felt sure Kimberly would come himself and get her. That would have had the Kimberly panache. But Annabelle had been impatient. She had chosen the classic end.

Farquar, now. Farquar would never risk his girl up in the firing line. And Chorley? There was a horse of a very different colour. When he learned that Philip Kimberly had risen from his grave in Leningrad, he would know how to use the girl. She would be Chorley's hostage. She would become his shield. Kimberly would not kill her. Not Philip Kimberly. That would not have style. Too Greek for him. And by then they would have their hands on him.

Knowing Kimberly as he did, Scaith believed he would gracefully throw in the sponge. Once his astounding cover was blown, he might begin to even enjoy this, his greatest of all jokes, bow to the victor and accept his punishment. A Kimberly through with the U.S.S.R., back in the fold.

Of course, he could never be forgiven. But he could be held in a comparatively tender trap. What Kimberly must know! Ah, the pleasurable hours that lay ahead!

Scaith brooded.

Chorley. Yes, Chorley. He was a tricky fellow, eager for awards. He would steal the thunder in the field. No question about that. This final accolade would fall to Chorley. He would know how to bring that about. Should a jewel not shine in Scaith's own crown? In fact, the biggest one of all?

Scaith had refused a Knighthood, gracefully, and thanked his Queen. 'Mander was enough for him, and to be allowed to serve.

Her Majesty had written him a personal letter and, when he was presented to her on the next official occasion, she had shaken his hand warmly

and called him 'Mander; without the C. But this
. . . this was different. Why should a man who
had reached the top of his profession be reduced
to the lowest rung of the nobility, become a
Knight? Kimberly . . . yes . . . this capturing of
Kimberly could make him a peer. Life peer, unfortunately. In any case, he hated his family, so
that would serve jolly well.

Only Cameron knew, and he himself. That was
how it would remain for the moment. The *reseau*
was on the hunt. They were after a Kuzminsky.
They might take him. But he—Scaith—would do
the ultimate unveiling.

Commander Scaith would personally declare
him as Philip Kimberly. Cameron and he. Yes, a
nice man with whom to be bracketed.

Suddenly, like a mosquito after blood, Scaith
heard a motor bicycle. The engine plooped and
stopped. After a count of six, his doorbell rang.
Instinct warned him to pour his fresh cup of tea
while there was time. He did so listening, providently withholding the lump of sugar.

Polly knocked and presented a special delivery
envelope. Scaith opened it and read the contents
carefully. He called his office number and ordered
an immediate check on all unidentified female
bodies under thirty years of age which had been
found during the last forty-eight hours.

Scaith stood up brusquely and reached for his
stick. First things first. He left the house and was
in his car before his tea had even thought of turning cold.

Penny waited in her flat for Ginger. She needed his moral support. Phil was not interested. He had hung up on her. He was out to save himself and that was all. There was a chance, she suddenly thought—not likely, but an outside chance —that Susan had gone home. Maybe her mother had followed her, which she had done before, pleaded her weak heart yet again, forcing Sue to fall in line. She was capable of anything to keep Susan at her beck and call. But the handbag? Sue still would not have gone without her handbag.

Penny looked up Susan's number. She listened to it ringing and heard the acid tone of Susan's mother.

"235–6583," she enunciated clearly.

"May I speak to Sue? It's—"

Before she could finish, she was interrupted.

"Susan has left home. I daresay she will contact her friends when she feels so inclined. But, in future, do not expect to find her here. She will be unwelcome, as will be her so-called friends. Good morning." The voice of doom cut off abruptly.

What a woman . . . what a bloody awful woman! Penny thought. She heard Ginger's taxi; the driver blowing his feeble horn. She ran to the window. There he was. She snatched her handbag, slammed the door and ran out to the lift.

Ginger had cut his face shaving. He was still dabbing it with a rather grubby handkerchief. Penny paid the fare.

"Ginger," she clung to his arm. "Come on up."

Before she led him through the entrance door, she saw the small green van again. It was across her own road. It was the same one that had been parked outside Farquar's house. Adrenaline pumped. It must be the one which had taken Susan. They discovered the mistake and now had come back for her! She ran, dragging Ginger to the lift.

Inside her flat, she slammed the door, hurried to the window and looked out. The van driver was speaking on a radio telephone.

"Tell me what's happened," Ginger said.

Penny turned to him. He appeared to have lost pounds in weight since she had seen him two weeks ago. She tried to collect her thoughts. How much could she tell Ginger? She looked out the window again. The driver was reading a newspaper. Penny turned back to Ginger in sudden decision.

"I'm in big trouble, Ginger. And I'm afraid my trouble has spilled over onto poor Sue. It will be difficult to believe it's true."

Ginger's face had grown grim, and he spoke raspingly.

"All right, Penny. What's happened to her?"

"What was supposed to happen to me." She fell into a chair, clutching her knees. She spoke earnestly, determined to get through. "You know me as Penny Black. But that's not really my name." Penny told him the whole story, omitting only that Kuzminsky the defector was in fact her

213

father, Philip Kimberly. "So he came to me with messages from Philip Kimberly. He was with my father when he died."

Ginger stared at her incredulously. "I don't believe a word of it!"

"I told you it would be difficult to believe. The man warned me the Russians would try to kidnap me if they thought he'd seen me. And that's what happened. Sue came here unexpectedly and they took her instead. They must have discovered the mistake because there's been a car following me since yesterday. That van outside."

Ginger strode to the window.

"That green van?"

"Yes. I think they've come for me."

The doorbell shrilled. They turned sharply to the little hall. Knocking followed the ringing of the bell.

"Oh, God!" Penny whispered.

Ginger put his fingers to his lips. They listened. They heard a key being inserted into the lock, listened to an abortive turn. The key was withdrawn. There was a brief silence. Again, they heard something thrust into the slot. This time it fitted and turned.

Penny gave a faint cry. Ginger gripped her arm.

Commander Scaith stepped over the threshold. Two large men followed close behind him.

"Miss Kimberly," Scaith said.

Scaith stopped abruptly and repeated her name

214

almost in wonder. Penny was the image of her mother, Annabelle.

"Yes," Penny said.

Scaith pointed his cane at Ginger.

"You must be Ginger Masters. Susan Peters's boyfriend." He turned to Penny. "Was he here with you this morning when you telephoned the man you called Farquar?"

"I haven't spoken to Farquar."

"Answer me, dammit!" Scaith struck the couch angrily with his cane. "Did he hear you make that call!"

"No."

Scaith turned to his men, gestured with his stick. "Take him downstairs. Wait in the car."

Before Ginger could voice a protest, he was quickly and gently armlocked and marched out of the flat.

"Please," Penny pleaded. "Don't hurt him. He doesn't know anything. He—"

"Miss Kimberly! You will tell me where—"

"No!" Penny looked at Scaith defiantly. "I'll tell you nothing! I'll speak to you when you bring Susan Peters up here. Tell your men to bring her up from that green van and I'll speak to you. Not before!"

"Van?" Scaith crossed to the window. "There's no van there now."

"Then—where is Susan?"

Penelope's false courage was beginning to desert her. Her question ended in a little cry for help, lip trembling. Scaith turned to her, frowning.

"Look here, Miss Kimberly. You know they have taken your friend Susan in error. I know it. *They* have taken her. Not *us*. It's thirty years since I've had to show my warrant card. But here it is." Scaith held the card up in front of her eyes. "Now, do you begin to understand? Sit down, Miss Kimberly." He indicated the chair he wanted her to use. He took a sheaf of papers from his pocket and selected an upright chair for himself. He began to read the transcript of her telephone conversation to the Bull Hotel.

"Phil. It's me. Penny. A girl came unexpectedly and let herself into my flat yesterday. Susan Peters. And she's gone. . . . Susan? Who is—I don't understand you . . ." Scaith looked up. "And so it goes on. He warns you not to go to the police, accuses you of being hysterical. Then, Miss Kimberly, he asks you where you are speaking from. Your own flat, you tell him. And what did he do, Miss Kimberly? What did he do then?"

"He—he hung up," Penny whispered, almost as though she were ashamed.

"Yes. Philip Kimberly, who knows your line must have been tapped ever since he came to me in the guise of Sergei Kuzminsky, hangs up. At once. Not one more word." He flashed another glance at her. "Your line was tapped, Miss Kimberly, to protect you, if necessary. And rightly so, I think you will agree. Now, then. Where was Kimberly when you spoke to him this morning?"

216

"I won't tell you," Penny said, but her mind was racing furiously, churning memories. Somehow, somewhere, she had seen this man before.

"Yes, Miss Kimberly. You will tell me. You will listen to every word I say and you will tell me. There is a constable lying at death's door in hospital, struck down by your father. And it is certain that he killed Professor Purloe."

Now Penny was again angry and defiant. "I don't believe you. I don't believe a word you say. My father . . . Phil . . . a spy, yes—but he is not a murderer! I'll never help you to persecute him!"

Again Scaith looked at her for a long moment, almost sorrowfully.

"I was with him on the towpath when he ran. He was pursued by Grierson. And he struck him down."

Suddenly, looking at the vulnerable young woman in front of him, Scaith felt an unaccustomed emotion: pity. He stood up abruptly, walked to the window. The unfortunate Ginger was down there in his car. Susan . . . yes . . . pity for them all. He returned and sat in his chair in front of Penny.

"Penny, listen to me. I've known your father for many years. I knew your mother. Annabelle. Knew her well. Your home called Wardrobes . . . I visited there many times when you were a little girl. I had a great affection for—all of you. When Kimberly defected, I did not turn on a hate mechanism. I gave him credit for being a cleverer man than I. But now . . . Philip Kimberly is no longer responsible for his actions. He is now dangerous. But I would still try to save his life. He may be shot down at any moment by the police or by his Russian—comrades. We must apprehend him as quickly and efficiently as possible before he *is* shot down. Or feels forced to kill again." Scaith paused, holding her eyes. "Tell me, Penny. Where is he?"

Penny shook her head in terrible distress and indecision.

"But—he warned me. Trust no one. How can I tell? You could be like Phil . . . working for the others. Looking for him only to kill him."

Scaith rose to his feet, snorting impatiently. "Do I look like a Russian fancier! Like anybody's bloody comrade! Chances are he left immediately after hanging up on you, but you must tell me where you called him!"

Abruptly, without further hesitation, Penny gave him the telephone number and the address of the Bull Hotel. Scaith's hand shot out like a claw and seized the telephone. He hugged it on his knees. He dialled the field office at Woburn Abbey and asked for James Chorley. He was not there. He called the office behind the Maidenhead hotel. He was told that Sir James had not been there and that Mr. Farquar had left for the Bull Hotel. There was news . . .

"I know the news!" Scaith snapped. He hung up. All roads were leading to the citadel. "We'll be on our way," he said to Penny. "Provide yourself with walking shoes and a warm coat. It will cloud over before the afternoon."

The fight had gone out of Penny. She rose and did as she was told.

Once more Scaith returned to the telephone. He reached his own office. "Any news on my search enquiry?" He listened. "Two. I see. Thank you . . . no, I'll not be coming in. I'll send instructions." He hung up. He stared through Penny, seeing another girl. "Susan?" he asked. "Is she easily recognisable? What would she be wearing?"

"Well . . . her best dress, I suppose, as she was running to see Ginger. She is very pretty."

"Very pretty. Yes. I see." Scaith sighed. "Let us go."

Ginger was waiting in the front seat of the car beside the driver. Penny made a pathetic attempt at smiling. The driver left his place and held the door for her to get into the back seat.

Scaith said something to him in an undertone before he climbed in awkwardly to sit next to Penny. They crossed London, going south. An outrider followed on a motorcycle. Over Westminster Bridge, they went by one-way streets and passed St. Thomas's Hospital. The driver pulled up at a large door in a bare wall. The outrider left his machine and opened Ginger's door.

"Where are we?" Penny asked.

Scaith forced himself to answer without hesitation.

"The City Morgue."

"But why?" She guessed the reason. "Oh, no!"

"Young man," Scaith said to Ginger, "there are two unidentified bodies in there—"

"You mean Sue might be . . . oh no, I can't?"

"Are you a man or not!" Scaith snapped. "Do you expect this lady to do your duty for you? Your young woman is missing. Do you or do you not want to know if she is dead? I've gone out of my way to bring you here!"

"I'll go with you, Ginger."

Penny reached for the door handle. She got out. The brilliant sun still lent a little hope.

"No need for you to expose yourself to this, Miss Kimberly."

Penny took Ginger's arm. "He's only a boy," she excused him.

"And you?"

"You know what I am."

She said it so bitterly that Scaith leaned back pretending he had not heard.

The first body they were shown was Susan's. One eye was half open, staring balefully. The other had been nibbled away by fish or water rats.

Penny gave a little cry. She dropped Susan's handbag.

Ginger whispered hoarsely: "Jesus!"

They went out together, leaving Susan once more united with her handbag. The brilliant sun was cold, a neon strip illuminating the horror they could never forget. Penny stood as though wondering where to go. Ginger vomited, leaning against the wall.

Penny found Scaith beside her, his arm supporting her elbow. "Come," he said. "My man will look after Ginger, get him a sedative and a car. Yes, we will take care of him."

Penny was back in Scaith's car, hardly aware Scaith was getting clumsily in beside her. They began to move. She turned her head. Ginger was still propped against the wall.

"Ginger," she called.

The man beside him made a small sign of understanding. Penny saw it and began to cry.

Scaith pretended not to notice.

Eleven

That same Good Friday morning, even before Scaith was visited by Cameron, Farquar left early for Maidenhead. The early sunshine already had warmth, promising a day to drive all thought of winter into the background of one's mind.

"For lo, the winter is past," Farquar repeated Solomon's Song to himself. "The rains have come over and gone."

So it was for himself and for Penny. She was a very lovely girl and he was the luckiest of men.

He found The Green Man in Maidenhead, drove round to the backyard, and parked. A man was already sweeping the steps.

"You are early at work," Farquar greeted him.

"So are you, sir. You from that lot upstairs? Coming and going all the night. Bit of excitement, eh?"

"Not too much, I hope. Where are the boys?"

"Upstairs, sir. Two floors on the right."

The field office, as at Woburn Abbey, had been

set up in a double room. Ordnance maps covered the two beds. Kuzminsky's picture stared at Farquar from the chimneypiece and the chest of drawers, propped up by Victorian pottery.

The men were drinking tea. They came to order. Farquar waved them to relax and took a cup himself. Each man made a report. Each report was negative. Farquar felt a small nerve jumping near his eye. He managed to control it.

"We'll simply have to carry on," he ordered. "It's early yet. People get about on a lovely day like this. Push. Get everybody on the job. See that each gate-keeper at Woburn Abbey has a photograph."

"We've got the gate-keepers organised, sir." The men offered Farquar a bunch of pictures. "Perhaps you'd like these for people staying at the house."

Farquar hesitated.

"I'd like to keep the house-guests out of it, if possible. I'll discuss it with Sir James Chorley, though we can scarcely hope to keep the matter covered for much longer. All this going on . . . I suppose the local coppers have been after you."

The man grinned.

"Oh, very curious, sir!"

"They would be. Well, carry on."

Farquar nodded and left. He was at the stair-head when a youngster hurtled past him and flung himself through the field office door. Farquar swung round.

"What's up, Connery? Taken short?"

"Oh! Sorry, sir," the young officer apologised. "Barging you like that. But I think we're onto him! He's—someone saw—they know the car—"

"Take a deep breath," Farquar said, and went back into the office.

A man who lived at Baker's End, doing the milk-round, had stopped, as he did every Friday, to drop off a pint at an isolated cottage. Sometimes, if the young lady was there, she gave him a cup of tea. If she wasn't there by Sunday, he poured the pint into a trough for the wild cats. The young lady thought they kept the mice at bay. She paid up once a month. This morning, the roundsman had found the door broken in: smashed and the wood all splintered. He went in to have a look.

Farquar tried to light a cigarette but fumbled his match. Somebody offered a lighter.

"What's the cottage called, Connery?"

Farquar drew deeply on his cigarette.

"Baker's End, I think, sir. No! Baker's Cottage. That's it: Baker's Cottage at Baker's End."

It was Penny's cottage.

"Did he find anything—anyone inside?"

"No, sir. Bit disorganised, he said. Not the way the young lady kept the place. But there was no one there. So this milkman, he pulled the door to, and told the policeman in the next village. There's no station at Baker's End."

The milkman hadn't thought much more about it. The damage to the cottage didn't seem extensive. He had decided it was probably a tramp looking for a comfortable night.

Farquar could visualise it all. Before he died in Moscow, Philip Kimberly had told Kuzminsky to bargain with Scaith. In good faith, he might have told him his daughter's whereabouts. The man had gone to the cottage, found the place locked and had broken in, looking for a safe and comfortable night. Thank God Penelope had not been there.

"Just a minute, Connery." Farquar instructed the man on the telephone to call his London flat. "So, Connery, you spoke of a car?"

"Yes, sir. And this is the bit of luck."

Connery started to explain the bit of luck but was interrupted by the telephone operator: No reply from Mr. Farquar's flat. Farquar nodded, glanced at his watch. Penny would be on her way to work.

"The car, Connery," he prompted.

"Yes, sir. This milkman, he's driving back to get on with his deliveries after reporting to the police when he sees this young lady's car. He knows it well. Many a time, he said, he'd pushed it down the lane for her when it wouldn't start."

"Where, Connery? Where's the car now?"

"I don't know, sir. But we have the number. And the milkman saw him." He pointed to the Kuzminsky photograph. "He came out of the Bull Hotel and drove off in this young lady's car."

Farquar felt a cold sweat of fear. There was menace here he didn't fully understand. Penny

226

had telephoned him at his office in London to put him off. She had said the cottage had suddenly depressed her and she was with friends at the Bull Hotel. But she had not mentioned a Russian, a Kuzminsky, and that she had left her car.

"Where's the milkman?"

"Downstairs."

"Fetch him up."

The milkman repeated the story he had told Connery. Seeing the strange man get into the young lady's car, he had imagined she had arrived, found her cottage broken into, and come for a bite of breakfast at the hotel with her friend who was on his way back to repair the door. In any case, he was behind time with his deliveries and had thought no more. He had done what had seemed necessary to him. It was while he was waiting to be paid at the café in town that Connery had questioned him.

"This gentlemen hauls over and shows me a photo. Well, he had sense. He knows I get about delivering milk. Nobody round here I don't know. And, even though he's a stranger, I recognised this man in the photo at once. Slanting eyes."

"What was he wearing?"

"Dark suit. A coat on his arm and carried a kind of chequered bag. He put it all in the car. He saw me, too, because I drove right by him to get to the back door of the pub to leave my milk."

"You really had a good look at him?" Farquar asked.

"Close on. Seeing the cottage was broke into, and him being in that car, I was curious. It's the man in the photo, all right."

"Thank you very much." Farquar stood up. "You've been a great help, and I'm sorry to have held you up. If you have any complaints from your employer, tell him to reach us here."

"Her. It's a her."

"Her, then. And we'll explain."

He offered his hand to the milkman, who shook it warmly.

"Thank you, sir. But there'll be no trouble. She's a good sort, her."

"The Bull Hotel," Farquar said. "Anybody here know it?"

"Passed it twice this morning," Connery said.

"Right. You drive with me. I want two men to follow in your car. He may have returned to the hotel." Farquar started out but stopped abruptly. "We don't approach the hotel frontally. He is dangerous. He may have acquired a gun."

Farquar led the way out of The Green Man. The milkman loitered. He tried to chat up the remaining occupant of the office.

"Dangerous, eh? With a gun? Who are they after?"

The telephone operator looked at him gravely.

"He's the chap's been robbing the school kids in East London of their jelly babies."

"Jelly babies, eh?"

The milkman hurried downstairs just in time to see the two cars drive away.

Kimberly had seen the milkman looking curiously at him. For a moment he thought he was going to hail him. He had braced himself, but the milkman drove into the yard of the Bull Hotel. Kimberly moved off.

Once out on the open road, a tremendous reaction set in. He had not wanted to attack the innkeeper, but Douglas had admitted listening to his conversation with Penny, and he was about to telephone the police. Kimberly had had no time for facile explanations. His time was beginning to run out. He was certain that Penny's telephone had been tapped. He must make for Woburn, but first he needed to change his clothes.

He was on a minor road with plenty of thicket all around, sliced by bridle paths. He chose one and turned into it. Even before he stopped his engine, two horsemen, cantering toward him, pulled up and ordered him back on the road. Kimberly apologised and reversed. They trotted past him on the shoulder of the road, making for another drive to let their horses go.

Kimberly had to force himself to act. The road before him began to move in slow waves, like a rolling sea, and he was only just able to get the car on the grass beside the road before he passed out.

He returned to consciousness very slowly. His head had fallen onto the steering wheel. He raised it heavily and leant back, waiting for strength to return and for his vision to focus properly. When he was able, he got out of the car. He struggled with his travelling bag into the wood.

Kimberly lay flat on the ground, ordering himself to rights. This could not happen to him. How could the accidental death of one man affect him in this way? His life had been full of necessary assassinations. In his world death was commonplace. Yet, this man? He had a feeling Douglas was grabbing feebly at his throat, fighting, begging to be allowed to live his simple, pleasant life.

Until now, Kimberly had been buoyed up by doctrine and ideals. But this had been in defence of nothing but himself. Well, he'd done it. Was he, then, a common murderer in his own eyes? The answer to that question could wait.

He sat up, unzipped his bag, found the wig he wanted. He took out the mirror, the glue, and the moustache. It was too late to question himself now, too late ever since those bastards had disfigured him and turned him from the pack. They would regret it. The thought of his revenge brought him strength.

He adjusted the padding beneath his shirt. He again chose the tweed coat and hat and the horn rimmed glasses. He slung the camera on his shoulder and brushed the grass from his trouser legs. He clutched his bag and went back to the car. He told himself the pain in his arm and shoulder would be enough to remind him not to pass out again. In fact, the short rest had done him good. He felt fit to plan and cope with his escape again. The next move would be to telephone

Scaith when he neared Woburn. He would arrange the meeting earlier and ask for a doctor to
be there. This time he would give Scaith the correct location for the rendezvous. It would be too
late by then for the new plan to be leaked through
the hole in the bucket to the K.G.B. He knew the
man who shot him the first night at Putney must
be the leak: someone close to Scaith, his weak-
link, someone who knew nearly everything. But
nearly was not enough. This time he, himself,
would pull the trigger. His arm ground with pain.

It would be a pleasure to point the gun and
squeeze.

Farquar drew up fifty yards away from the
front of the Bull Hotel. He called to the men in
the second car to drive round the rear. They
were to patrol the riverside and the back door.
Connery would cover the side entrance.

It was not yet opening time, but the daily servants were busy preparing for the Easter rush.
Farquar saw someone polishing silver in the dining room. Upstairs, a Hoover moaned. Pauline
was at the reception desk, speaking into the telephone.

"I am sorry. We're fully booked. All the rooms
are taken. Yes, we can manage four for dinner
on Saturday, but Sunday lunch is taken up. We
do have nice snacks at the bar and we have a
lovely lawn and boats. . . . Yes, I understand . . .
if the weather lasts. Thank you for inquiring."
She hung up, raised her eyebrows to Farquar.

"Yes, what can I do for you?"

"Are you the proprietor?"

"The wife—Mrs. Ransom, yes."

"Could I have a word with your husband?"

"I can't find Doug anywhere. Really, it's too bad: leaving me with the rooms and doing the flowers and answering the 'phone. . . ."

Farquar produced Kuzminsky's photograph.

"Mrs. Ransom . . . is this man a guest here?"

"Well, he's gone, too. His car has gone. He probably took Doug into town, but he'll be back any minute. It's not like Doug to leave the place before the help arrive."

"He left the place alone?"

Suddenly Pauline Ransom tightened up. "You're a bailiff, aren't you? After that poor man! Well, you may as well leave now. I won't have people served with writs! Not in my hotel!"

"Mrs. Ransom, I'm not serving a writ." He dropped his voice and tapped the photograph. "You may be in trouble."

"Trouble? You must me joking! Penny Black brought him. He's a gentleman and a friend of hers. Though—" She broke off, remembering Doug as she had left to buy her flowers "Though my husband did say they had an argument this morning."

Penny brought him! The phrase kept repeating itself in Farquar's head. Why hadn't she told him?

"Was Penny here today?"

"No. She telephoned. She hasn't been here

since the day they came." Pauline turned up the hotel register. "Wednesday. See?"

She pushed the book towards Farquar. There it was: his own name in full with his address: booked in on Wednesday. He closed the book and passed it back to her.

Farquar tried to work it out. Kuzminsky had obviously gone to Penny, much as he had gone to Scaith, and asked her to keep a secret for her father's sake. He had made up a story to appeal to her. Penny had brought him here in good faith, kept her secret, and gone off. She had probably rung this morning to arrange to pick up her car today. Since he was supposed to be in Switzerland, it would help Penny to fill in time and get her car back. Kuzminsky had a rendezvous at Woburn. The argument must have been to do with that: Kuzminsky wanted to keep the car. Yes, it could work out that way. But Farquar was frightened. Who had broken down Penny's cottage door if Kuzminsky had been safely here? A tramp? The milkman thought so.

"Mrs. Ransom, you say your husband Douglas was alone here with this man?"

"Must have been. He hadn't had his breakfast. And I left Doug getting a cup of tea."

Farquar hesitated briefly before speaking again.

"Mrs. Ransom . . . is there anywhere this man could have locked your husband up? If— say—there had been an argument? Suppose he wanted to get off without paying."

"But he was loaded! Not when he first came because we lent Penny twenty pounds. Look here, we've been talking as though you know Penny."

Farquar nodded. "I do."

"Then you know she wouldn't be involved in any funny business. He paid back the twenty pounds from a big roll. From his solicitor, I think it was."

"Wish my solicitor would give me a big roll!" They both laughed. "But is there anyplace—a broom cupboard—?"

"The maid's been in there."

"Anywhere else?"

Pauline looked at Farquar gravely for a moment.

"You're serious," she said flatly.

"I'm afraid I am."

"Well, there's the—listen, now you're getting me scared!"

"There's what, Mrs. Ransom?" Farquar said quietly.

"The cellar. But I'd like to see anyone lock Doug in his own cellar!"

"Where?"

"Here. Right here. It's a trapdoor."

"I'd like to bring one of my men in, Mrs. Ransom." Farquar went to the side door. "Connery. In here, if you please." Connery came in, wiping his feet. Farquar dropped his voice to a whisper. "The boss is missing. There's a cellar. I think we ought to have a look."

Pauline was already struggling with the trapdoor. Connery came to her assistance.

"Let me, ma'am."

Connery lifted the door and propped it back against the wall, showing a ladder leading down. Pauline began laughing.

"Come on, Doug. We know you're down there drinking up the profits!" She shrugged impatiently.

Connery looked at Farquar.

"Shall I?"

"There's a light switch," Pauline said. "Rummage round. And don't you go drinking the profits either!"

Farquar tried to edge Pauline Ransom away from the trapdoor.

"You're all booked up for Easter?"

"Yes. Hope the weather keeps."

They heard Connery coming up the cellar steps. Farquar knew at once.

"There's been an accident," Connery said.

"No!"

Pauline screamed and pushed towards the ladder. Connery held her back.

" 'Fraid he's dead, ma'am. Must have fallen down."

Pauline was struggling to get past. She could now see down the ladder.

"There's no one there!"

"In the corner. Covered by those sacks."

"Oh, my God! Doug!"

"Call the boys in, Connery. We'll bring him

up. . . . Mrs. Ransom, you need a brandy."
Pauline's screams had brought everyone running
to the hall. Farquar explained quickly. "Mr.
Ransom has had an accident. Take Mrs. Ransom
to the kitchen. Get her a drink."

Everyone did as Farquar ordered.

Douglas Ransom was hoisted from his cellar
and laid on the polished bar where he had drunk
so many glasses with his friends and been a gen-
erous, sympathetic host. Someone covered him
with a sheet until the ambulance arrived.

Pauline, her face taut and white, was back on
the telephone. Doug's dad was on his way round.
The pub had once been his. He couldn't see it
closed for Easter. They would never let the public
down.

With the local police now arrived and in
charge, Farquar said good-bye to Pauline Ransom. She stared at him blankly, her mind screened
of the man who had brought her the bad news.
Then it came through. Her lips trembled. Farquar
took her hand, squeezed it.

"You're being very brave. Mrs. Ransom . . .
is there anything about the man he couldn't alter?
If, for example, he dressed up, disguised himself,
is there something I could tell him by?"

"His hand," she said. "A big scar straight down
the palm. Devil's scar. He killed my Douglas
with his hands."

"Thank you, Mrs. Ransom."

Farquar hurried away.

Polly must have been polishing in the front room because she had the door open before Scaith got his keys out.

"Well, what's this?" she said. "Nice time of day to come home, and no warning. You'd think we had a full staff!"

Scaith gave Penny an encouraging push into the hall. "Here's a young lady, Polly. She's had a nasty shock. Nothing she wants to discuss with you, I may add. But take her into the kitchen and give her a cup of tea. Some of your nice anchovy toast. I'll give you a call when I'm ready to have a chat with her."

He saw them both through the kitchen door. "So you've had a shock, eh? Poor dear. Tell Polly all about it."

Scaith banged the floor with his stick. "No gossip, I said!"

He left them and stumped off to his own room. He got through to his secretary at his office.

"Where have you been?" she asked.

"Burying the dead."

"Ah, Christ! So that missing girl is dead." She sighed deeply, but became brisk again at once. "There's a lot of signals come through. One on the four-zero line. But the gentleman wouldn't talk. Will ring again. Said he wants to make the meeting earlier."

"He'll have to wait my time!"

"Don't we all?"

"You're very uppity today!"

"You're not here with your big stick," she tittered.

"That's enough!" Scaith snapped. "Let's have the signals."

He listened while she read them out. There was one from Farquar at the Bull Hotel. Scaith ordered his secretary to get him through to Farquar at once. She had the line cleared to the Bull Hotel and connected Scaith, in his Putney house, via her office in Whitehall.

Scaith's call was too late. Farquar had already gone. Connery asked permission to speak. Scaith listened without comment till the end.

"Thank you," he said, and listened again. "Yes, Connery. Stay there with the local police. Listen and say nothing to them. Wait for orders. Help that poor woman any way you can."

He hung up. So Kimberly had killed again. He had cold-bloodedly murdered the man who, however unwittingly, had sheltered him.

He called Penny to his room and offered her a chair. For a moment, he felt incapable of telling her of this latest crime. It seemed to put a barrier between them once again. How could he now call her Penny? A child's name? Bad. The affair was going badly.

"Miss Kimberly . . ."

"Yes?"

"I'm sorry to have to tell you this: Philip Kimberly has killed your friend Douglas Ransom."

"No!" Penny cried out. "Doug? Oh, no!"

"Killed him. Threw him in a cellar and is now

on his way to Woburn Abbey where, presumably, he had hidden his stolen goods. He must now feel terribly threatened. He may run wild. He could decide to kill the Duke or take the Duchess hostage. Anything. What was to have been a simple exchange of money for safe conduct from the country and the delivery of certain files has become a very dangerous operation. It could clearly be suicidal now to trust Philip Kimberly to keep his part of the bargain. And I do not want a blood bath. He may even have prepared an ambush for us in Switzerland. There are any number of men who can be bought and he knows—"

The little telephone rang: the four-zero line without number or dial. Scaith took it up before it could ring again.

"Scaith here." He listened, looked at his watch, and continued to listen. Finally he spoke. "Understood. Now listen to me: as from the end of this call, this number will be discontinued. I am reading you back for the last time. You say you are in need of a doctor. We will provide one. The exchange of money will be in the church at the main gate at Woburn at four o'clock, and not in the children's zoo as formerly arranged.

"The messenger will come to the back seat on the left, facing the altar. You will check the money. You will then go with the messenger to the official car. The doctor will be there to treat you en route to the airfield. If necessary, he will accompany you on the flight to Geneva. There you will be supervised throughout the night. Arrangements have been made for the bank in Geneva to open for us tomorrow morning. The sum you ask is on deposit. And there the final exchange of documents will take place. Understood?" He listened for a moment. "Agreed. One further change of plan. This time, mine. The messenger will not be a man wearing a red handkerchief. It will be a female." He looked at Penny: "She will be dressed in grey with a grey and white spotted blouse."

Scaith hung up and kept his eyes fixed on Penny.

"That was Philip?"

"Yes."

"You mean to send *me*?"

"I think he will hesitate to kill you."

"What makes you think so?"

"He has never killed a woman in his life."

"Except my mother!"

"No, Miss Kimberly. No." Scaith sighed. "We killed her. We. I and the rest like me."

Penelope sat in heavy silence, unwavering eyes on Scaith's sombre face. "When it's all over," she said quietly, "when you've made your exchange, however you do it, what will happen to Phil?"

"He's built his gallows extremely high, Miss Kimberly."

"You said you would try to save him."

"Save him to be finished off, thrown into a pit, riddled with K.G.B. bullets? I can save him for that, yes, if it's your wish. But, with your help, I mean to get the file and hold him. He will spend the rest of his life in a prison of a sort. Surely a better alternative than the pit."

"Any sort of prison for Phil would be worse than dying!"

"Miss Kimberly, do you want to deny the man time to repent?"

"Repent?"

"For Susan. For your friend Douglas Ransom. For the innocents."

"Are you a religious man, Commander?"

"There are a few sharp corners that never will rub off. I find them most uncomfortable at times."

"Except times like this when you use them to bargain."

"Are we bargaining?"

"Oh, yes." She sat forward in her chair. "Yes, I am now bargaining. I want Philip Kimberly to stay dead in Leningrad. But you will save this man Kuzminsky. Let *him* do the repenting. Do you understand?"

"I am listening."

"None of this was done by Philip Kimberly. I will help you if no one ever knows—ever guesses —this dreadful end of a man who, at least, followed his own star. There I am a spy's daughter. I can keep my silence as well as you. Philip Kimberly died in Russia. They killed him. You know that. That's my bargain. I will go into that church and do what must be done as long as Philip Kimberly stays in his grave. Agreed?"

Scaith stood up awkwardly. "Agreed, Miss Kimberly." He came round the table and took her hands. "I understand you, Miss Kimberly. It is what I would wish myself."

Penny sat up, trying to look very tough. "I could do with a strong drink."

"I could do with one myself. But Polly wouldn't like it: a young lady like yourself drinking in the morning. We'll be on our way and stop off where we won't be seen."

"You really are a strange old man, Commander Scaith. I could have got to like you."

"Perhaps so . . . perhaps so . . ."

"Will you be at the Woburn church? Will you stay near me? If you can?"

Scaith looked at her for a long moment, and, again, he saw the face of the one woman. "Miss Kimberly," he said softly, "if it were possible, I would stay near to you until the crack of doom."

Penny stood up, preparing to go. There was no answer to this.

"Just one minute, Miss Kimberly. I must begin to fulfill my part of our bargain." He used his telephone. Penny listened while he ordered a doctor and an ambulance. "To treat a case of septicaemia," he said. "It's to wait opposite the church at Woburn Abbey. It will be there from one o'clock. And the attendant will be armed with a narcotic gun. That's all."

He turned to Penny.

"Forearmed," he said.

When the phone clicked to final silence after his talk with Scaith, Kimberly knew the arrangements were now irrevocable. He was familiar with the system. The line had been put into operation for himself alone and was probably already scrubbed.

He wondered why a female operative had been chosen. The old man must have his reasons. In any case, Scaith must have access to a safe house in Geneva with ultimate security. He would take advantage of the doctor's treatment and a full night's rest. When he was assured the money was irrevocably his in a numbered account, he would disclose the hiding place at Woburn.

He knew he would be held at the safe house in Geneva until this was verified. Once they had the microfilm in their hands, they would let him loose. He would be of no further interest to them. He would then go willingly to hospital praying to save his arm.

Through all this, his three passports beckoned like victory flags.

Because of Kimberly's fainting fit, Farquar was catching up and following close behind. He would have overtaken him if he had not felt impelled to take a loop road and go himself to see Penny's cottage. There was a possibility that he, as a trained observer, might notice something the milkman had not seen or, if he had, had not understood as significant.

Farquar stopped at the front door of the cottage. It was intact. He walked round to the back, saw Penny's clothes pegs gathered in a bag and felt something of her presence. The smell of her linen dried in the open air had an aroma of its own. Her hair, fresh from its rinse in rain water, made her more desirable than any woman he had known.

All through the last year, in spite of their affair, she had preserved a quality he had not been able to touch: not, that is, until the Wednesday night when they had both abandoned themselves, all barriers down, and made their promises for good.

He saw the broken back door. It filled him with disgust. It was a kind of rape. This was not the work of a passing tramp. They had a country cunning. They could break in without a trace. In general, they were not an unwholesome breed: they slept, brewed up their billy-can and passed on, leaving a sign for others who would understand and make use of the place as well. No damage would be done.

Farquar stepped closer to the door. The lock had been blasted off by a revolver shot. A boot had finished the job. Farquar knew at once: Soviet agents, close on the scent of their defector, had done this, and no one else. If the K.G.B. were as close behind Kuzminsky as this, there could be competition for him when they moved to pick him up. He went into the cottage to have a quick look around. Thank God Penny had not been there when the men had come with guns.

The place had not been ransacked. A search had been made only of those places where a man might hide. Cupboard doors were open, upstairs a bedcover torn away, and in the storeroom a stack of old trunks had been tipped and thrown over. Nothing more.

There was a photograph of himself on a chest of drawers, and another of Penny's parents in colour. He picked it up, studying Kimberly. It was the face of a rather ordinary man. He could see Penny's eyes but they were surrounded by indelible lines. They were not the lines of dissipation or of fun. They were lines traced by perpetual strain.

Farquar looked at his own reflection in a mirror. There were signs of the same lines gathering. But no more. He promised himself: his term of duty was coming to a close and that was that. He and Penny would take off.

He hurried downstairs, barricaded the door as best he could, and drove on. He was now anxious to find Chorley, whether Chorley wanted him or not. He had had a feeling all along they had been too complaisant about the efforts of the K.G.B. to recapture their man. How strange. If it had not been for Penny taking Kuzminsky to her friends, he'd have been in Soviet hands long ago. In her own way, without knowing it, she had done a great service. The British still had a better chance of pulling off the deal because of her. One of these days, she would probably confide in him. He would be vague, pretending not to fully understand. Poor little Penny with her sweet-smelling hair. To have a father as a double agent was enough. Her husband would be an ordinary man.

He drove on, once more nearly on the heels of Kimberly.

Kimberly had stopped to pick up petrol. He was about to pay when another car, driven by a pretty girl, pulled in to ask the way. The garage attendant pored over the map with her. By the time she felt sure she knew where she was going, Kimberly had been waiting some minutes to get on.

Farquar was running short of petrol himself. He stopped at the same pumps to reflll shortly after Kimberly had left. Before he paid, he pulled out the Kuzminsky photograph.

"Seen this man drive by or stop in today?" The man had not. "You are sure? He would be driving an old Mini convertible."

"I had an old Mini convertible in just now. But the gent driving was an old grey-headed man. Not him in that photograph."

"Keep the change!"

It was fifty pence. The garage man knew there must be a mistake, but Farquar cut out in front of an oncoming car and stood on the accelerator. The car behind him screeched in anger on its brakes.

On his last excursion into Woburn village, Kimberly had noted a field of stored tractors, farm trucks, and ploughs. He turned in and stopped behind a hedge to pick his spot.

Farquar flashed past.

Kimberly reversed close to a van covered by a

tarpaulin. He pulled this sheeting over his car and walked into Woburn, carrying his bag. He stopped at the Bedford Arms while Farquar was upstairs, telephoning to the field office in the Abbey.

Kimberly booked for lunch. He said he wanted to take a walk and asked to leave his bag. He left, carrying his camera.

Farquar got Chorley on the line.

"Well, Farquar, we're making progress. You turned up that dead body fairly swiftly. Didn't give the poor sod time to cool. Well done. But there's still grass to cut!"

"I'll be round at once. One urgent matter. The car we want passed through Woburn village not many minutes ago. It may have got into the park or be up a side street. Kuzminsky might be wearing a greyish wig and looking old. That should be added at once to the A.P.B.

"From the horse's mouth?"

"I try not to make unnecessary mistakes."

Farquar packed his bag.

Twelve

Kimberly sauntered up the main street, looking like any other man taking a day off. He glanced in the shop windows and listened to the church bells. He followed them all the way.

The congregation was gathering but, as the vicar had foretold, the great turn-out would not be today. There were perhaps three dozen in the nave. Kimberly noted with satisfaction that, in his gentlemanly clothes, he blended in, as though he went every week to morning prayer. Nobody turned curious eyes on him. He followed the service easily. It had scarcely changed since he was a boy in school at Harrow-on-the-Hill.

Harrow-on-the-Hill . . .

"There is a green hill far away," the congregation sang. "Without a city wall. . . . Where our dear Lord was crucified. . . . Who died to save us all."

The vicar gave a short address. He, too, was saving himself for the third day.

"And on the third day, our Lord rose again from the dead . . ."

He spoke quietly. He believed every word he said was true.

Kimberly believed him. There were some men you could not kill. He was one of them. He let his eyes stray to the marble sarcophagus from which his microfilm would be resurrected by tomorrow.

Maybe there was something in what the vicar said. No sin was unforgivable. Yet, could one lay off like that? He thought of the years he had spent in mortal fear. Maybe he was paid up in advance.

The service was drawing to a close. The congregation were preparing to receive the sacrament. Ladies tucked away their gloves.

A tight band seemed to encircle Kimberly's head and squeeze. The mystique was unacceptable. The service went on.

"We do not presume to come to this, Thy table, O Merciful Lord, trusting in our own righteousness, but in Thy manifold and great mercies."

There was a great sense of expectancy in all the church.

"Almighty God, our Heavenly Father who, of Thy tender mercy, did give . . ." The vicar took the bread, blessing it, then the wine, "Drink ye all of this, for this is My blood of the New Testament."

What about the Old Testament? Kimberly

thought. The jealous God. The God who destroyed the earth by flood. The God who turned that poor, curious bitch, Lot's wife, into a pillar of salt.

The vicar tasted the bread and wine himself, and gave the Communion to the young curate who was assisting him. The congregation shuffled in their seats. They were invited to approach the altar rail.

Everyone in front of Kimberly rose up and filed towards the flickering candlelight, toward the flowers where the Lord's Supper would be served. The first row of communicants knelt down. The vicar's voice was low, intimate, reaching to each soul in turn.

Kimberly could not catch the words. By now almost everyone was standing in the aisle. The first, already blessed and forgiven their sins, were returning to their seats. He forced himself to his feet. He would be conspicuous if he, alone, refused the sacrament. There was only one woman left to follow him. As he got closer to the rail, his head began to swim. He heard the vicar's words spasmodically.

"Christ died for thee. Feed on Him in thy heart."

There was an empty space at the altar rail. He fell on his knees, holding to the wood. He had to prepare his hands to take the wafer. Somehow, he managed it, and then the wine. The white napkin wiping the chalice . . . the chalice itself . . . seeming disembodied and floating before his eyes . . . and turned into the face of Douglas Ransom and the voice from somewhere . . .

"The Blood of our Lord Jesus Christ . . . shed for thee . . . and be thankful . . ."

Kimberly held the wine within his mouth and then swallowed. He was back in his seat. He knelt and then stood while the congregation sang. He received the benediction with them, and he followed them outside.

Farquar was once again admitted to the main house by a plainclothesman with his own key. He was taken upstairs. Today the house was teeming with sightseers kept in orderly lines behind red ropes, guiding them through the famous state rooms open to the public.

Farquar saw the pleasure and interest on their faces. He wished he were having a day off instead of dealing with James Chorley which, he felt, could only be embarrassing to both of them. He found Chorley comfortably ensconced in the second room, feet up on the double bed.

Chorley waved him in.

"You've put out a search for the car?" Farquar asked.

"Oh, indeedie! Bloodhounds on the scent. It's becoming very exciting isn't it? He's got the carrot, not we." Chorley clapped his soft palms together. "Interesting. Fascinating man."

"A very dangerous and irrational man. And we ourselves: haven't we been a trifle unrealistic about the powerfully hard muscle of the K.G.B.?"

Chorley left his reclining position on the bed. "We? Who is we?" His lower lip stuck out. "Every known agent has been under constant observation. They are growing sullen and discontented in Kensington Palace Gardens. Even the Ambassador has a satellite in his wake. Our so-called diplomatic relations are crumbling to the lowest, cunning exchange of lies. I do have friends at the Embassy. I have done my best. But charisma can only stretch so far."

Chorley stalked the room, back and forth, between the window and the bed. Farquar's eyes followed him spellbound. In his bathroom the previous night, Farquar had seen a man of muscle covered with fur. Now, he could visualise a long, prehensile tail taped to Chorley's leg. He was the epitome—if such a thing were possible— of man's regressive journey back to monkey, the whole enclosed in splendidly hand-woven tweed. Yet, he did have magnetism. It was not impossible he did carry weight in the ponderous atmosphere of the Soviet Embassy.

Farquar pursued his point. "You've had the report on the break-in of Miss Kimberly's cottage. So you can see why I believe the K.G.B. were on Kuzminsky's heels when he found cover at the riverside hotel."

"They lost him there."

It was a flat statement. Yet Farquar still felt obliged to stress his fears. "We should expect heavy opposition when we attempt to pick Kuzminsky up."

"Unlikely." Chorley was totally unimpressed. "In any event, we will be prepared. I have not been playing Idle Jack, you know! I have forty of my best people, male and female, mingling with the crowd. All armed. We do not expect trouble. But even if the K.G.B. do show their shining red faces, they will never succeed in taking our man from us." Chorley's voice grew clipped. "Item: two armed helicopters. Item: machine guns mounted on four private cars and on two innocent-looking farm vehicles. Item: Air Force providing a very special machine to whisk Kuzminsky to their airstrip. And, as Scaith explained, we will travel with a fighter escort to Geneva." He seemed to have suddenly used up all his steam, all his muscle melting into fat. "But I am a portly old man, as you no doubt observed with distaste when I did you the favour of visiting in private. An effort to make friends. However, people often fail to understand me. Portly . . . old. I can no longer run like a mountain goat. I want you there. I depend upon you."

Farquar heard it as a genuine plea.

"As long as you have no intention of using all these weapons. That operation is primed for overkill. Someone could get caught in the cross-fire. I'd hate it to be me."

Chorley snatched Farquar's hand, pumping it up and down. "Thank you, Farquar. Defence has not yet ceased to be the foremost method of attack. And may I remind you I possess a Military Cross and a D.S.O. with Bar. I have seen much action. But I am not ashamed to ask for your helping hand."

He released Farquar's fingers. Like a child with jam on them, Farquar wiped his fingers upon his coat. Ten minutes later they left the house.

Farquar and James Chorley walked through the playground, stopped by the merry-go-round and threw hoops over objects on the hoopla stand. Chorley was very skilful, precise, ringing every time. They made their way slowly, Chorley indicating his small army.

"This is our dry run," he said. "Kuzminsky sees us here for the first time. He follows to the zoo, which is over there."

Chorley played the sightseer with enthusiasm. In the children's zoo, he rhapsodised about the baby goats, and bounced away to the kiosk to buy them food.

"Here. Exactly here," he said, pointing. "We leave the money bag. One of my men will be inside the kiosk as a sales clerk. He hands the bag to you. You drop it. Kuzminsky picks it up. Then—unless there is interference—we follow him. If the Other People attempt to move, we call in help, by which we are surrounded: the man in the cloth cap carrying that basket: armed with a Thompson. He's been ordered to fire low, of course."

"I am glad to hear it."

"There are others. We are well covered. You will be sporting the red handkerchief. Once you drop the money, you lead up that rise, straight to the helicopter. I will be in the rear guard, accompanying him from there."

When Kimberly left the morning service, he walked blindly into the park, one of many enjoying the Easter sun. He chose a place to rest where he could still hear the church clock sound the hours. He sighed as he lay down.

Where had it all gone wrong? What had become of the strong young man, prepared to carry a world's burdens on his shoulder? He recalled, years ago, lying on his back in a field not far from where he rested now, watching Spitfires streaking overhead.

He remembered watching a dogfight and the moral stab of pain he had felt when one had splintered like a firework before falling in a screeching streak of smoke and flame. That pilot had died young, still confident that his life and effort and his death were all worthwhile.

Could he say that? Poor Kimberly. He felt himself to be outside, looking down on the body stretched on the sweet-smelling grass. That was poor Kimberly who had nothing left but pain. Leave him to it, poor sod, and walk away. Somewhere there was a place to start again; somewhere young men were eager, ready to sprint and win a race. He would join them. Good-bye, Phil.

The sleeping body stirred, agony snatching it back from coma. The eyes opened and swept the sky for warplanes. The ears, concentrating, heard only the murmur of bees.

He sat up and propped his back against a tree. This would never do, drifting involuntarily away into a semi-conscious state. It was nothing but the stealthy march of poison, festering and spreading from his arm and reaching like a glutton to devour the whole of him. Fortunately, this was an enemy he could understand and fight. And Scaith had promised him a doctor.

The church clock struck an hour and then two quarters. He got to his feet. All that was demanded of him now was self-discipline.

He walked a hundred paces, counting them, and stopped to rest. He realised he had left his camera on the grass. He would return and find it and take some photographs, but he misjudged the distance and the tree. It became a matter of immense importance—he had to find the tree. He had walked a hundred paces. He counted them. Surely he was still able to count up to a hundred!

The decision whether to retreat the numbered paces and begin again, or to continue searching under other trees nearby, seemed to swell in importance, like a toy balloon growing paler as its substance stretched until it burst. He stumbled, took an instinctive step to save himself, and there it was, under his feet. It was new and shining, purchased only yesterday.

He picked it up. His left arm was almost useless. But the mechanism of the camera was simple. He managed to turn the handle. He watched the dots and then the pointing finger carefully. The number one slid into the window.

Like a birthday child in possession of a grown-up toy, he wanted to use it immediately. An oak tree and a clump of rhododendrons in full bloom were begging to be snapped, but he swivelled round toward a longer shot. Woburn church filled his viewfinder. In his feverish mind, everything fell into focus then.

The nightmare had begun when Boris handed him his own obituary. He knew immediately he was a dead man: his years of service scrubbed, wiped off the slate as though he had never planned and schemed and devoted himself without thought of personal gain; as though he had never abandoned all, hungered, and risked his life for the cause. To gain time, he had pretended to poor Boris he believed the type-set obituary to be a heavy-handed joke. The strait-jacket, however, had put an end to that.

From that moment, as they chopped and stitched, he was a different man. The change was not only physical. When he learned their goal, he knew he had them in his hands. Somehow, if he lived long enough, he would kill Purloe and deliver the Soviet paymaster's files into Scaith's hands.

It was justice.

Swaying, staring into the viewfinder, he saw only that this had to be the truth. He had made a terrible mistake. But he was eager to make amends. His flight from the Foreign Office and his visit to Scaith had been but a preliminary game—the fondling of lovers parted too long—the researching for each other before the comforting return to the old place in the familiar bed.

Unconsciously, he must have always intended to make his gesture in the church where he had left the Soviet files. The money and the bargaining and the talk of Switzerland whirled in the mist of yesterday. That, too, had been part of the ritual dance before surrender. There had to be human sacrifice. The people who had been in his way had, of necessity, been swept aside. His sins had been forgiven him. In the church that morning . . . in the church . . . he was growing more confused. In the church, he'd thought that he himself was Jesus Christ. That was not really so —though of course he had himself been crucified.

He clicked his camera on the church. Everything was falling into place. He had his picture. He began his slow walk back towards his meeting place.

Farquar circled the park twice. The tourist activity in the stately home had extended everywhere. The world and his brother were enjoying it all. Since one thing he was searching for was Penny's car, she was on his mind. He decided as soon as Operation Grim was concluded, he would have to make a personal appeal to Scaith. Penny could not be held responsible for helping Kuzminsky. A stranger arrives at her door, bearing deathbed messages from her father. What was she supposed to do—turn him out? Scaith must stretch a point. He had Farq, the well-known scapegoat, to chastise if he felt vindictive. But why should he?

Scaith's career, which had been tailing off— the Prime Minister uncertain how to lose the irascible old man with dignity—would end in a blaze of glory. He would be amongst the comets of professional spies, seen only once in fifty years and disappearing, shrouded in mystique. He would have the glamour of a Kim Philby, say, without the smear.

Farquar made his way back to the Abbey. This time, he took his gun from the locked compartment of his car. He found a Chorley who had lost all his *sang-froid*. He was in a state of tension, smoking steadily, studying his watch and pulling on his lower lip. He made a great deal of unnecessary fuss about the red handkerchief Farquar was to wear. Farquar had folded it and tucked it discreetly in his breast pocket, a thin line of scarlet showing.

"What's that supposed to be?" Chorley snapped. "A *Légion d'Honneur?*"

Chorley snatched the handkerchief, rearranged the cloth, and thrust it back like a bouquet.

"I hope you're not setting me up for the target!" Farquar plucked the red handkerchief out again, making a compromise. "I'll leave enough to fire at." He grinned. "Right above the heart."

He looked at his watch. "Time to move on, Sir James."

The men looked at each other, as though it were a final measuring of strength. The phone shrilled in the sudden silence.

"Take it, take it!"

Chorley's voice had risen a tone. Farquar answered it. He listened, visibly perplexed. "Just a moment." He turned to Chorley. "Did you know that Commander Scaith has an ambulance stationed at the main gate? This is from London Centre. There's a hangup somewhere. The driver's waiting for instructions."

Chorley shrugged impatiently.

"Not our pigeon."

Farquar again spoke into the phone. "If Commander Scaith has sent an ambulance and doctor to stand at the main gate, he must have his reasons. The man will stay there until he is recalled. Tell the local constable."

Farquar hung up. Both men left the room. In the outer office, Chorley picked up a camera case which contained a walkie-talkie. He emitted a brief signal, received his answer, and headed for the lift. Each one of the office staff knew better than to say good-luck. Each one knew there was an arsenal outside, yet, even among themselves, no one spoke of it. At this late date, someone had learned how to spell the word "security."

Fifty percent of the visitors to Woburn had eaten lunch, washed down by beer or gin-and-tonic. The sun was high. Everyone was in good spirits. The children took advantage of the general goodfellowship to hold out their grubby paws for more.

"Just one more go! Oh, be a sport! Please?"

Even some of the parents took to the old-fashioned merry-go-round, and Uncle This or That was carted off to spend his savings on the fun.

Farquar and James Chorley walked through the crowd, like spectators at a feast. No one seemed to notice them. Unexpectedly, Farquar stopped dead in his tracks. Chorley heard him whisper "Christ!" and Chorley echoed him.

The Duke and Duchess of Bedford were walking together across the fairground, toward the Antique Gallery. They were sauntering at their ease, pointing out the sights to friends. They were observed by the crowds of visitors who hurried after them for autographs.

"Actually, it's for the best," Farquar said. "A counterattraction. Gives us more space." Farquar touched Chorley's arm and they moved on across the fairground. "Here we are. Buy yourself a bunch of hoops. I'll show the flag."

Farquar loosened the red handkerchief and let it flutter. He revolved slowly. He brought the red handkerchief to his nose and replaced it in his pocket. He walked casually round the hoopla stand, stopped for a moment to watch Chorley's unfailing aim, and returned to where he started from.

By now Farquar knew he had given the watcher plenty of time to observe him. He began his walk towards the children's zoo. There he also took his time, making the complete tour before going to the kiosk. The man selling food for the small animals handed him a leather case. Farquar took it and put it on the ground.

As it had been rehearsed, he walked on, threading his way towards the car park and the heliport. Farquar presumed Chorley's forces were bringing up the rear with the Russian and his loot. In the distance he heard the merry-go-round hurdy-gurdy begin its cycle of tunes over again. He headed directly for the armoured Air Force helicopter, its blades idling, ready for immediate flight. An Air Force Pilot officer looked down at him.

"Anti-climax, eh?" he said. "Here I am, hoarding brandy like a damned St. Bernard dog, and not a shot fired in anger. What a sell!"

Farquar turned round. Fifty yards behind, Chorley was advancing up the hill, carrying the leather moneybag. When he reached Farquar, for all his weight, Chorley was not out of breath. Farquar noted he was not as unfit as he had said.

"Tipped off!" Chorley snapped.

"What do you mean 'tipped off'? He made the arrangements, not us."

"Someone must have leaked he was not going to get away with this—this free ride to Switzerland!"

"That was Scaith's bargain."

"But not *mine!*"

For a moment, Farquar studied Chorley's face

gravely. "Then he is wiser than I thought," he said quietly. He looked up to the pilot officer in the helicopter. "I can only say we're sorry you've been troubled." He turned back to Chorley. "I'll be off. Good-bye. I have retired from the Service as from—" He glanced at his watch "—two-forty-five today."

Farquar turned and strode away. He wanted to run. In an odd way, he felt he had been mocked. Yet, not by Kuzminsky. The whole operation, since Chorley entered it, had the smell of fake. But now he intended, in his own way and in his own time, to discover why.

His BMW was standing by the main entrance of the house where he had left it with the windscreen shattered. And who the hell had done that? This, too, he intended to find out.

The shattered screen had been removed but not replaced. He looked at the Jaguar with distaste. He transferred his bags to the boot of the BMW and put down the folding top. If he was going to travel in a draught, let it be a gale. He shrugged on an overcoat, found sunglasses in the pocket, and turned on the engine. At least he was his own man now, in his own car. He roared away too fast, flinging up the gravel.

Families which had come early and had far to go were beginning to make tracks for home. Farquar had to slow down and get in line. He grew impatient. Once more he took the side road, a track leading past the lake. He arrived at the main gates from behind the church and saw the ambulance.

Scaith had ordered the ambulance. Why? That was the first thing he would find out. He was waiting for an oportunity to edge into the traffic on the main drive outside the church when he saw the man stumble in the graveyard. He had been taking a photograph when suddenly he toppled over. It looked as though he had fainted and cracked his head on the granite stone of a grave.

Farquar jerked his car to a standstill, left the BMW, and vaulted over the wall within ten seconds. He bent to help the man. He was clutching at the gravestone but there was no cohesion in any of his movements.

"Here. Let me give you a hand."

Farquar slid his hands beneath the armpits of the man. His offer was received with a polite but stubborn refusal.

"Thanks. I will be all right." His words slurred one into the other. "Stumbled."

Farquar thought the man might have taken a little too much Easter wine. By now he was on his knees, slowly struggling to stand up.

"Sure you are all right?"

"Perfectly, thank you."

He dusted himself and produced a key from his pocket. Farquar picked up the camera.

"Your camera, sir."

'Very kind. Thank you." The man nodded and turned away. "Meeting in the church," he said.

"Easter. We pull out all the stops. . . . Church warden's work is never done. . . ."

Farquar took a few steps after him toward the small western door. He watched him insert the key and let himself in. In the doorway, he turned and raised his hand in a small gesture of gratitude and farewell.

Farquar saw the scar. In a few strides, he was at the door. It closed firmly in his face. He tried the handle. The door was already locked. In seconds, he was around the church and at the main entrance. A huge key was in the lock—by Scaith's command, no doubt. Farquar turned it. Crouching in the shadow of the great door, he inched forward.

The man with the scarred hand passed by the altar rail and vanished through a small door leading to the vestry. As this second door closed, it struck Farquar he might be mistaken. The man had a badly scarred hand, yes, but he had spoken with a distinct English accent. Very U, indeed. Certainly no trace of Russian. But Scaith's ambulance was there.

Seemingly unrelated incidents pinwheeled through Farquar's mind: failure at the arranged rendezvous with the Russian, a man with a scarred hand, Scaith's ambulance and Scaith's repeated insistence that the microfilm must be delivered into his own hands. The clear conclusion: Scaith trusted no one and had planned to collar the maniac by himself.

Farquar felt a sudden, strange filial fury to-

wards the older man: how dared he risk himself
. . . alone . . . limp into battle!

Farquar moved silently into the church,
stepped over the altar rail, and listened at the
door. He heard the gushing of tapwater, the
scrape of tired feet, and nothing more. Since
there was no outside entrance to the small
eastern vestry, the man must come out through
the same door or stay inside.

Farquar hesitated: he could go in and take
him, hold him for Scaith . . . but—that English
accent . . . what if he was wrong? He decided to
retreat into the body of the church and wait,
ready to support Scaith if it should become necessary, yet leaving him the prize, if there should be
a prize.

Farquar mounted the steps leading to the gallery and studied the situation from there. A swift
look from a south window—scarcely more than
an air-vent hidden by one of the huge groined
ribs supporting the roof, showed the ambulance
still stationary. The driver and the man beside
him were smoking. The rear was curtained off.
Scaith had to be in there, smoking too, while his
much too private plan simmered, waiting to boil.
Farquar could not help admiring the stubborn
courage of the old man: uncertain of whom to
trust, lonely on his pinnacle, he had decided to
make the final move alone.

From his window, Farquar saw he was perfectly positioned to cover Scaith, both inside and
outside the church. Like the others, he, too,

would have to wait, but without benefit of a cigarette. He leaned his shoulder blades against the wall, trying to draw a little granite into his system from the ancient stones . . . enough, at least, to see him through his vigil behind the groined rib.

Thirteen

During the last three days, James Chorley and Farquar had lived mainly for the capture of Kuzminsky. Although they had been together only spasmodically, spiritually it was as if they had eaten the same meat from the same plate and drunk deeply from the same cup of wine. They were obsessed by the one desire of dedicated professionals.

For two nights, they had dreamed the same dream. It was therefore a natural sequence that they should wake to one reality within minutes of each other, just as two men of equal calibre pondering a problem will normally arrive at the correct solution at approximately the same time. Almost as Farquar saw the telltale scar, light dawned on Chorley, piercing the clouds of his frustration and rage. Now, he saw clearly why contact with the Russian had come to nothing: Commander Scaith had intended the operation to abort!

Scaith must have set up a different meeting place. He intended to take the defector by himself, possess the microfilm, the honour and glory, and rid himself of the traitor in his camp.

While Chorley's mind raced, his body functioned swiftly. He hailed one of his armoured cars, dismissed the driver, took his place and drove off, bounding over the rough ground towards the ambulance placed by Scaith.

The church clock began its chime and beckoned Chorley. He knew he was right. Like an airplane circling in the dark and flying blind, he had been signalled in to land, talked down by the bells.

Lurking inside the empty church—each second, slovenly to pass, seeming to take a minute —Farquar suddenly felt he had been discovered: a Jonah in some monstrous stomach, the ribcage bellying above, sporadic sounds caused by the heating system suggesting gases and digestive juices plumbing the organs and entrails of the beast who had him caged. Then the church clock immediately above his head attacked his eardrums, ringing the quarters and the hour.

Farquar counted slowly.

Kimberly had doused his face under the tap in the choirboy's washroom. He abandoned his heated blood to its ice-cold shock, loosening the spirit gum so that the moustache fell into the basin.

With fingertips, as though it were an insect, he flung it to the floor and scrubbed it with his shoe. He clawed at his upper lip. Bloodshot eyes glared back at him from the mildewed looking-glass. He was affronted by the stranger's stare and turned away with dignity.

He saw the vicar's surplice and dog collar hanging on a hook. He painstakingly fastened the collar around his neck and pulled the surplice on. He turned back to the mirror defiantly: no one would mistake this grey-haired preacher for Philip Kimberly. He knew this for certain; for he had done it all before.

Philip Kimberly had left England from this church ten years ago. He and his wife Annabelle had driven there from Piers Purloe's house. They had hidden the microfilm in the same cache they had used during the war years for passing messages. Their parting had not been sad. It was exciting. They were off to fresh fields. Their apprenticeship was over. Philip was to go to Moscow by the underground route. She would wait in Switzerland until he found it safe for her to travel with their child. The microfilm would be their passport, an insurance policy paid up for life.

They had embraced and she settled the surplice on his shoulders and pulled his lips down on hers again. He had grabbed her convulsively, a sexual quality in his hunger at their last embrace.

"None of that," she had laughed, a warm chuckle in her throat. "You are a priest—behave

271

like one. I'm going out to make sure no one is about. Wait five minutes. Take the car. And go. I've got the torch. Don't fall, for heaven's sake!" She turned at the door to look at him once more. "I won't come back," she said quietly. "We'll meet in Moscow." And, for the last time, she vanished from his sight.

Now Kimberly started back into the church as the last echo of the clock died away. Farquar heard the vestry door opening. He sank himself against the masonry as though he were a bas relief and watched the priest.

Above the altar, above the crucifix, above the crown of thorns, light from the oriel window spilled down on Philip Kimberly.

From where Farquar stood, he saw a strangely exalted, almost disembodied, man.

The clock had finished striking. Commander Scaith left the ambulance. Penny followed him. He handed her a leather satchel. She hung it on her shoulder and squeezed his arm, a warm last-minute contact before she crossed the road and went, without hesitating, to the main entrance of the church.

When Farquar saw Penny approach, his heart stopped beating and then raced abominably, as though to make up time. What was this? He saw Scaith follow more slowly, kept waiting by impatient cars, and he heard Penny fumbling the key he had already turned.

Commander Scaith edged slowly into the

church, clothed himself in the shadow of the great carved door, and watched. Penny looked only in the direction she had been told to go. She was to wait in the back seat, on the left-hand side of the church, facing the altar. Her heels clip-clopped on the slate floor. She reached the pew, hesitated only a brief split-second before she slid in and sat on the hard oak plank. Custom, as well as fear, made her lean forward to offer a prayer.

"Make it all right, please God. Let it work out all right for Phil, and comfort Ginger and Pauline and . . . and . . ."

She sat back, her eyes staring until they fell, with relief, on the clergyman; but when he stepped down from the altar rail into the nave, she saw that it was Kimberly.

His face had shrunk in the two days. The emaciated face and robe made him look like an El Greco Christ. He was a frightening figure. He leaned resting against the pulpit steps, gathering strength to walk down the aisle. He reached the flying angel just beside her. She stood up and he saw her.

His vivid memory leaving Annabelle—and sight of his daughter there at the meeting place —jolted him.

"Penny? . . . Penny! What are you doing? Who told you—who brought you here?"

"Commander Scaith. He had my phone tapped. He heard me speak to you today. He came for me. He means to do well by you. That's why he asked me to bring the money here myself. And a doctor. The way you wanted. The doctor is waiting in an ambulance and—"

She was stopped by the tortured screech of brakes, intruding through the church door like an obscenity.

Farquar had not been able to hear what Penny had said, though the name "Scaith" seemed to reach his ears. It came like a bad scratch on a gramophone record. He heard no more until the same sound which had halted Penny pulled his attention to the main door. He saw Scaith move a short step forward from the no-light to the half-light where he paused again, leaning heavily on his stick: a moment in time when nothing moved.

Kimberly stood stock-still, scenting trouble.

Penny, motionless, a ghost of a girl, was a perfect image of her mother: any moment, and she would again fade back to the grave.

Scaith remained a graven gargoyle.

Farquar, in the gallery, a medieval God, gun in hand, preparing to hurl thunder.

The thunder came from the church door: Chorley came through it like a tank. Only Scaith's stick, miraculously swift, deflected his aim: the bullet tore into the flying angel, leaving a gaping hole, and sparing Kimberly.

"Kimberly!" Scaith roared. "Get down!" He struck out again at Chorley viciously with his stick, knocking the gun from his hand. "Save yourself, Kimberly!" he roared again. "Out the back door!"

Farquar, crouched low and partially protected by the heavy wood of the gallery, was concentrating only on finding the right moment to get Penny into safety. Scaith had put her in the firing line: treating her like a soldier, using her surname . . . using her! He edged his way closer to the staircase.

Kimberly had drawn his own revolver, pulling Penny in front of him. Now everything was clear to him again: he had been tricked! Safe conduct and a doctor! His own daughter was there to cheat him, but he knew what he had to do.

Kimberly twisted Penny's arm behind her, forcing her to be his shield. Even his wounded arm responded to his last and greatest effort to survive. Pain was a thing apart—one rose above it when the moment came. He forced her nearer to the flying angel, holding her between himself and the others in the church.

"Hear me!" Scaith shouted. "Don't be a fool! I am your friend. The money is there. The doctor and the plane are waiting. This gunfire is not my doing!"

Kimberly's shot slammed into the folds of the flying angel. Another great chunk of marble was dislodged. He pushed Penny closer, crouching and fully covered by her body.

"Reach into that hole. Take the package." Penny was too terrified to move. "The bastards tricked me! Take it!" Penny reached into the crevice. She touched the package. Her fingers closed on it. She withdrew it from the hole. "Now! Move on with me!"

"Throw it here!"

Scaith had never shouted louder in his life. Penny would have obeyed, but she was stopped by Farquar's voice:

"No! Don't do it, Penny! Kuzminsky is a killer!"

She let out a brief cry: "Farq!"

"Do exactly as he says or he'll kill you!"

They had all looked up to the gallery. Chorley turned to Scaith.

"Farquar! Your precious traitor! We have him now!"

Even under threat of Farquar's gun, Chorley took a step toward his own to see Scaith's black, highly polished laced shoe planted solidly on it. Scaith shouted once again: "Let me have it, Kimberly!"

But Philip Kimberly was pressing Penny forward with his gun. He knew no one would fire at him. Even from his vantage point, the man in the gallery would be afraid that, during the violence of death, Kimberly's finger might clench on the trigger and the girl would die as well.

Yes, Kimberly felt safe: he knew these men. He approached Scaith and Chorley slowly, and, with his gun, waved them silently aside.

This was the only moment Farquar could have fired, but Scaith's eyes reached him, a small shake of his head forbidding him to kill. The old man obviously still had something up his sleeve. The moment passed. The gun once more menaced Penny's back.

Scaith and Chorley were now both beneath the pulpit, with Kimberly backing toward the main door, Penny his perfect shield, perfectly in place. He paused by Chorley's gun, kicked it violently to send it snaking down an aisle. The sound of metal on slate, amplified by taut nerves, sounded like a dying scream for help which would never come in time.

Now Kimberly had Penny out of the church. The great key turned and his enemies were locked inside. He remembered the BMW from which Farquar had jumped behind the church, the keys dangling in the ignition. He prodded Penny, ordering her towards the car.

Inside the church, James Chorley, once more the human tank, hurled himself against the great carved door.

Farquar tore to the side entrance, but Kimberly had removed the key. He fired at the lock, slammed his body against the splintered wood, and raced from the church.

Chorley turned, swept past Scaith, and found his gun lodged beneath a back pew. He grabbed it and followed Farquar.

"I hold you responsible!" Scaith screamed after him. "You and Farquar!" He was shouting to an empty church. "He would never, never have harmed the girl!" His scream of rage and frustration echoed back at him.

Then there was silence.

Dust of centuries, dislodged by gunfire, was falling lazily, caught like scarves of finest net and lit obliquely to pale rainbow colours by the descending sun.

Scaith was alone. His rage was monumental. The microfilm should have been in his hands. Everyone had bungled. There was still a chance Farquar would recover it, but Kimberly or the girl might be the price. If only he had been left alone! He would have dealt with Kimberly. They had been friends. He understood the subtleties of his defection. The tremendous loneliness, and having no one left to respect, must have driven him to drink with obsession. Scaith had only to hold out his hand for this wounded outcast dog to lick it. But the bunglers had driven the dog mad!

Scaith picked his way across the church to the flying angel. He looked at the inscription on the raised plaque at the pedestal:

"To the beloved memory of . . ."

The bullets had torn the rest away. Scaith's mind was bursting with obscenities.

To the beloved memory of shits, of traitors, of fornicating fools undeserving to be called Englishmen! How many coded messages had been passed on from this same obscene anti-sacred hiding place!

Scaith put his hand into the cavity. Suddenly the statue moved. After Kimberly's gunshot, this last aggression tumbled it. Almost in slow motion, it teetered until the balance gave. He stepped back. The angel crashed into the aisle, throwing up another cloud of dust.

Scaith pulled out his handkerchief and trumpeted his nose. The dust was making his eyes water. He scrubbed at them with his knuckles, like a child weeping.

Fourteen

Penny had driven Farquar's BMW many times before. Now, ordered by Kimberly, the gun pressed into her side, she raced the car across the open country, bucking like an untrained horse.

Farquar had commandeered a Section motorcycle from Connery and followed her.

James Chorley ran for his car. He followed Farquar's trail.

With Kimberly crouching beside her in the open BMW, Penny could only assume he knew where he was going and that they were being pursued. She felt sure that Scaith would try to help her. And Farquar. Farquar? God knew how or why, but Farquar had been there in the church. He would certainly be following if he could find a car.

Penny heard a motorcycle, glanced sideways for an instant, and hit a bump in the uneven ground. The car bounced and swerved almost a half-circle so that it was facing downhill again.

Kimberly jabbed the gun into her ribs, his voice rasping.

"Just you bloody well shut up!" she snapped, suddenly angered by his bullying. "I'm doing my best. If we go on like this, we'll lose a wheel. And I personally don't give a damn!"

She changed down and began climbing the hill again.

Once on the summit, Kimberly saw a copse ahead. He reached across Penny and swung the wheel, turning the car sharply so that they ran steeply down the other side of the hill they had just climbed.

Penny fought him for the wheel, aiming for a track with a side road crossing in front of them. She skidded round, crashing a heavily loaded dray carrying animal food. Their wheels appeared to lock. Crates of fruit and vegetables catapulted into the BMW.

Kimberly, now driving right across Penny, managed to swing the car loose and stamp his foot on hers. The needle mounted on the accelerator once again. They tore round a corner and crashed through a gate which a game warden, a war pensioner with a wooden leg, was opening to receive the evening meal. He made a stalwart attempt to halt the careening car, but was left cursing in the dust, his artificial leg destroyed.

Sheer impetus carried the car on into the centre of the wood, but the steering had been damaged. They continued on helplessly until they struck a tree. They had penetrated deeply into the Monkey Wood. Hundreds of animals started chattering excitedly.

Farquar had seen his BMW swerve onto the cross road. He decided to traverse the slope instead of following directly. From halfway down the hill, he had seen the game warden savagely mown down. Then he saw Chorley's car in close pursuit, closing in on the entrance to the wood.

Farquar was not sure if the animals were dangerous. But with Penny held by Kuzminsky, and a gun-happy Chorley on their heels, he decided to get into the wood as quickly as he could. He rode past the injured game warden, promising that help would be on its way. He left the motorcycle, and ran through the undergrowth to where he heard an increasing sound of frantic animals.

Inside their territory, the monkeys had held back, screaming furiously at the careening open car, but when they saw it held their evening meal they descended on it greedily, all anxious to be first.

Kimberly tried to fight them off. Infuriated by his aggression, screaming and scratching and biting, the monkeys overwhelmed him, submerging him beneath a wave of fury. Kimberly screamed in terror. Penny tumbled out of the car, onto the leaf mould. A small chimpanzee clung tightly round her throat.

Chorley's car pulled up and Penny ran to it. The small chimp sprang from her, scampering back to the source of food.

'Help him, help him! The monkeys. They're killing him!"

Chorley fired two shots into the petrol tank of the BMW. The car burst into flame. The fire threw the animals into further panic. Chattering and screaming hysterically, they retreated to the trees.

Kimberly managed to throw himself from the car, his flowing vicar's surplice a flaming torch. He rolled himself into the damp undergrowth, tearing at the cloth to free himself. Blinded by smoke, he struggled to his knees, fumbling for his gun.

Penny saw Chorley's revolver steadying on the window ledge of his car, pointing at Kimberly. She screamed and struck at him as he fired, but Chorley's bullet managed to find Kimberly. He returned the fire from his knees, catching Chorley in the chest just as Farquar broke through the underbrush.

"Stop! Hold it!" he shouted.

Chorley swivelled round, aiming point blank at Farquar's heart. He squeezed the trigger, winging Farquar in the left shoulder as the gun fell from his fingers and he crumpled over the steering wheel.

The blazing car had set fire to lower branches. A great chimney of black smoke rose through the centre of the wood. Tongues of flame leapt high.

Commander Scaith's ambulance forced its way down the woodland track toward the holocaust.

Farquar stepped into its path, fearful that it, too, might blaze. The driver threw his gears into reverse and backed away. Farquar followed him.

Penny, frozen for a shocked moment, saw the tattered remains of Kimberly's gown rekindle like a child's squib thrown independently at a firework display, after the big set-piece had been sent up. She left the car and ran to him.

"Phil! Phil!" She beat the growing tongue of flame with her bare hands. Kimberly opened his eyes wearily, saw a canopy of green and smelled the smoke. The flame killed, Penny knelt beside him and raised his head onto her knees. "Phil?"

Kimberly responded lazily. "Bloody smoke." She nodded silently. "Listen. Can you hear me?"

She understood he could not hear. "Yes," she whispered.

"So sorry. Didn't intend you to get involved like this. Old Scaith, was it?" Again she nodded. "Well, there you are. Too bad. Not your fault. Sorry about that girl and your friend at the pub. War is bad."

He raised his right hand to her face. She took it and put her lips against the fatal scar.

"Love you," she muttered.

"Your man . . . Farquar . . ." he said.

Penny, alerted, eyes wide, tears falling, listened. But Kimberly was tired and sank back into oblivion. Penny never heard what he was going to say.

People crowded around them.

Kimberly was moved into Scaith's ambulance. Scaith stood outside staring bitterly at the burned out car. He spoke to no one. Finally he followed Kimberly into the ambulance. Penny roused herself and caught the door before he closed it.

"Commander . . . is there any hope that he will live?"

Scaith stared through her.

"Can't tell," the doctor answered. "We will do our best."

Suddenly Scaith found his voice. "It's of no consequence, Miss Kimberly. All our efforts, our hopes, all the loss of life . . . wasted. All gone up in smoke. You did your best." He turned away. "Drive on."

Although bleeding freely himself, Farquar had been helping settle Chorley in a second ambulance. Now he came to Penny. They looked at each other for an instant. "You're badly torn by those bloody apes," he said quietly. "You must get to the hospital for anti-tetanus serum. Your hands—they must be treated. I'll come on as soon as I can."

Farquar saw her eyes had turned to agate. "Why?"

"Why? Because . . ." His throat was suddenly parched. He raised his arm to wipe his eyes and smeared his blood-soaked sleeve across his forehead.

"You're bleeding," she said. "You'd better go in the ambulance. I will be all right."

She toppled over in a faint and was carried to a car.

Farquar went in the ambulance with Chorley. They were forced to stop at the main gate. Farquar saw one of his own men.

"Connery."

"Sir?"

"Bring my Jaguar round. It's outside the big house."

"Yes, sir."

"Follow to the hospital. I'll stay with Sir James."

The ambulance attendant touched Farquar's blood-stained sleeve.

"You won't need no car tonight, sir."

Farquar simply gestured Connery to take off.

James Chorley's colour was not good, but he seemed to be emerging from shock. His eyelids flickered. They closed and flickered again, and this time they remained open. Farquar had never really noticed the colour of Chorley's eyes before: they looked like polished jade, pale green. He whispered something. Farquar leant close.

"Paul?"

Farquar laid his good hand over Chorley's.

"Yes. Paul. He was quite a guy."

It took Chorley some time to recognise Farquar.

"If you had to take him from me. . . . If you . . ." A tear trickled from the jade-green eyes. "Why did you let him down?"

"James . . . your lines are crossed. Paul was

never anything to me. He was a good friend. Brave. A marvellous agent."

Chorley made an effort to sit up.

"But he wrote to me. Got his letter here." His hand wandered to a non-existent pocket and fell limply on the blanket. "Said he'd found another friend. A man. But in the end . . . last letter . . ." Again Chorley's hand began to search. "Said a woman . . . she got between . . . so he killed himself."

"No. No, James. Nothing to do with me. The woman was the fellow's wife. The man we got the ciphers from. The man from the U.S. War College. They both died. He and his wife. Incredibly sad. All three of them. Far too decent for our game. Cut out. I understand it."

"The man from . . . *that* was the man?"

"Yes, James."

"Oh, God . . ."

Chorley stopped struggling to sit up. He fell back on the coarse cotton pillowcase.

"James—listen." Farquar bent close to Chorley's ear, whispering. "It's no good. You must forget. The man's dead, too. We can't go looking back."

Chorley sighed a long, slow sigh. His time was running out and he knew it.

"Yesterday . . . when I fired at your car . . ."

"I know, I know."

"I tried to kill you."

"Damn near succeeded."

Farquar felt a feeble grip from Chorley's fingers.

"I'd have killed anyone for Paul."

"Well, there you are. Rest now."

"Farq . . . and after all . . . after all this . . that damned portfolio went up in flames. Too bad."

Farquar sensed a surprising complaisance in his words. He studied the shadow of a smile on Chorley's lips.

"You set the car on fire, didn't you?"

"Oh, yes. Yes, indeed, I set the car on fire."

"Well, we mustn't worry about that now."

"You're a very bright young man, old Farquar. I am sure you know why I set the car on fire. The portfolio would have made very interesting reading."

Farquar nodded his head gravely.

"You were working with the other people."

"Since 1937."

"With Kimberly."

"Ah, yes . . . ah, yes . . . and we were let down by the bunglers."

"You knew of this operation from the start. And you had to try to kill Kuzminsky the day he got away. You couldn't let that list fall into our hands."

Chorley tried to nod.

"The bunglers . . . the bunglers . . . ah, if we hadn't been let down . . . did Kimberly die?"

Farquar thought the clouds of death had penetrated, bringing peace at last to his disordered mind.

"Yes, James. On Monday. In Moscow."

"No, Farquar, no!" Chorley became impatient. "It was Kimberly all the time. We faked his death. Remember I went to Istanbul late last year? But I pottered on to Moscow. We arranged it then. It nearly worked. But then he got away. A better agent than you'll ever be, old Farquar. We were all fond of Kimberly. Scaith and Masterman and George and . . . old George . . . he's dead, too . . . shame. . . ."

"Kimberly? Philip Kimberly? Kuzminsky is . . . ?"

"Of course, Farquar, of course . . . very imaginative, don't you think? My idea, really. All of it . . . I've been a very successful man . . . very clever man. . . ."

Now the silence lasted a long time. When they reached the hospital, Farquar gently adjusted Sir James Chorley's wig and told the stretcher bearer he was dead.

After Farquar had his arm plugged and dressed, he asked what had happened to Penny. He was told she had been taken in and was being treated for wounds and shock and no one was to see her.

"I am her fiancé."

After consultation, the senior sister led the way upstairs.

Penny was in a small ward by herself. A hospital gown was tied closely round her neck.

"Penny?"

She opened her eyes. "I thought you'd come," she said.

"Of course I'd come."

She sat up, fumbled beneath her pillow, and produced a package.

"You wanted this." Farquar made no move and he saw her eyes were still agate. "Take it. It's what you wanted all along. You had a long haul, Farq, but you did your duty. You kept in touch with Kimberly's kid." She flung the package to him. "Does it feel good? Was it worth a whole year of going to bed with me? Was the whole thing worthwhile?"

"Penny . . . please listen to me. I didn't know. And the whole thing will be worthwhile when we marry. We didn't hurry our decision. We waited a long time."

"You waited until Philip Kimberly came back to England. You had your orders and *that's* how long you waited!"

"You can't believe this, Penny. Did Commander Scaith tell you this?"

"He didn't mention you. You'd done your job. You'd kept me on ice. Why should he mention you? No doubt he'll give you the kudos you've earned in person. Now, take him his rotten microfilm. I am tired . . . so awfully tired. . . ."

Her voice was thin, weary of the thoughts behind the words, and weary of the words themselves. She turned her face away.

Farquar knew that any minute she would say

good-bye and, knowing her, he knew it would be final. He forestalled her, saying an abrupt goodnight, and left her there, strangely anonymous— a patient in a hospital ward.

Outside the hospital, Connery waited in the Jaguar. He jumped to hold open the door of the back seat for Farquar.

"No, Connery," Farquar said. "I'm going to the Abbey. I'll drive myself."

Although Connery was conditioned to taking orders, he raised a small protest as Farquar slid behind the wheel.

"But—your arm, sir."

"It's all right. Got a lift yourself?"

"Yes, sir. The place is stiff with local constabulary. They're very curious, sir."

"That's the way to keep them, Connery. Curious. Not a word."

Connery nodded seriously. Only as Farquar drove away did Connery realise how little he knew of the war they had waged today. He was very curious himself.

Farquar drove like an automaton, pondering the details he did not understand. How, for instance, had Scaith inveigled Penny into the showdown at the church? That would take some explaining. He would squeeze the truth from Scaith, even though he was a lame old man.

And Kimberly. How long had Scaith known that? He must have known for some time that it was Philip Kimberly. He kept it to himself. If Scaith had told him, he would have recognised the danger to Penny at once. Her flat and her cottage were the first obvious places to be ransacked by Soviet agents trying to recapture him. And Scaith had withheld the news!

Farquar promised himself he would get the truth from Scaith before he handed him the microfilm.

He stopped at the Bedford Arms in Woburn village. He explained his friend had been injured and was in hospital. He wanted to take some things to him. The manager handed him Chorley's key.

Farquar went upstairs and let himself into the dead man's room. There was very little to pack. He did it methodically. He found the letters from Paul Ives. He found a few photographs: Paul and Sir James Chorley. He tore everything in half and stacked it in the fireplace. He was just bending down, setting fire to the first leaf, when Commander Scaith stomped through the bedroom door.

Farquar automatically stood up. Scaith stalked over to the fireplace.

"What are you burning?"

"Personal papers."

"There are no personal papers in our trade!"

"Personal letters when a man is dead."

"Chorley? He is dead?"

"An hour ago in the ambulance."

"All gone." Scaith glared at the papers in the fire. "Years of planning. All up in flames."

He raised his stick as though to bring it down in anger across Farquar's back.

"You are a shit," Farquar said quietly.

Scaith looked faintly puzzled. He lowered the stick, a wand without potency, and then it came to him: Farquar was thinking of the girl—of the girl and not of the microfilm cremated in the car. He gave a short, dry bark. Hah! So when the girl had found out Farquar's involvement, she turned him out into the cold. Somehow, to Scaith, the girl and the mother were synonymous. To him, it seemed that it was Farquar who had possessed them both . . . and he, neither.

He leant heavily on his stick and thrust his face aggressively towards Farquar.

"We are all shits!" he said.

Suddenly Farquar kicked viciously at Scaith's cane. He fell sprawling to the floor.

"But you are a lame shit," he said.

Scaith pulled himself up by the bedpost.

"You're finished!" he rasped. "Finished!"

"I have already given notice of my retirement."

"Retire? Hah! You're fired! In disgrace!"

"As you wish."

Scaith slammed the door as Farquar turned his back on him to tend his little funeral pyre. He felt viciously glad he had withheld the microfilm. Scaith would have to sweat with rage and frustration another night.

There was one more photograph he had missed on the bedside table. He slid it into his pocket with the microfilm. He finished packing Chorley's clothes and carried the bag downstairs. His arm was giving him trouble. Although he knew it would aggravate the pain, he went into the bar and bought a large whisky which he downed in a gulp. He went to the desk to pay Chorley's bill.

Chorley's private car stood outside, empty as a hearse waiting for a coffin. Farquar put Chorley's bag in the boot, got into the Jaguar, and drove away. An impulse made him turn into the grounds of Woburn Abbey. He would begin his new life now. He would take a drink with pleasant people living in a civilised world.

Before he rang to enter, he walked over the dank grass for half an hour, trying to find repose. This time he was let in by the butler. The Special Service men were gone. Life in the stately home was back to normal.

Farquar was led upstairs to the drawing room. Commander Scaith was there, taking up the centre of a sofa. Farquar saw him from the door and stopped.

The Duke and Duchess both stood up to welcome him. He was the hero of the hour, lucky to have come out of the fray with his life. The room was full of exclamations. The Duchess was anxious for her wounded friend to have a seat. She led him to the sofa, insisting he must stay the night. The room used for his office was empty and waiting. She would not be refused.

"Make room," she said to Scaith. "You must meet each other: my good friend 'Arold Farquar, and this is Puppy Scaith."

Scaith's eyes met Farquar's, daring a comment.

Farquar sat down. Scaith was muttering something beneath his breath. Farquar had to lean across to hear him.

"Been to the hospital. Seen Miss Kimberly. Advise you to return tomorrow when we've all had time to rest. Felt I owed it to her to explain. That girl, very keen on you. Very keen. Though God knows why."

Farquar, surprised, looked at him with raised eyebrows.

"A Scaith with a conscience?" he whispered.

Scaith snorted. "Probably regret it the rest of me life!"

Sometime later, during the general conversation, Farquar pushed a small oblong packet across the damask cushion to Commander Scaith.

"For you, sir. From Miss Kimberly. She saved it from the wreck."

Scaith needed no explanation.

"And you, sir," he said, "will get a C.B.E."

Farquar retired early. He was back in the room where Chorley, very much alive, had sprawled on the bed only that afternoon, planning his last mischief.

Farquar fished in his pocket and put Paul Ives's photograph beside the bed. He looked at the youthful face for a moment and sighed. In the end, one death had brought about the other.

Now that everything was over, he was incredibly tired. He was filled with a sadness he had never known before. Poor Paul. He thought awhile of Paul, but fortunately his arm began to throb and he was able to put his total weariness and melancholy down to loss of blood.

He turned out his bedside light.

Tomorrow, he would go back to the little hospital and visit James Chorley in the morgue. One must respect one's enemies. What was it Scaith had said? He might also be allowed upstairs again to speak to Penny.

Tomorrow . . .

That would be tomorrow . . .

For a while, he knew that he might have to live from day to day. . . .

Epilogue

Winter had been abrasive.

Lord Scaith of Glentarnock, Life Peer on his retirement, had chafed his hands before the smokey fire built of local peat. The evil Scottish mist had invaded the double windows and the impregnable walls of the fortress, attacking the empty sleeve of Sergei Kuzminsky as though his arm still hung there festering. Scaith's maidservant, Polly, commandeered from Putney, found the steep stone stairs almost beyond her.

Thus they passed the winter, the jailer and the jailed, each prisoner of the other. And, like the Ancient Mariner, each had a tale to unfold. So they drank and told interminable stories, working on their past lives like a giant jigsaw puzzle, many pieces failing to fit.

But, at last, spring had crept into the glen. Lambs were born. Sergei Kuzminsky patrolled the rampart with his field glasses, looking for the return of migratory birds and, especially, for the advent of official cars again, now that the road was free of snow. When this happened, he would retire to his apartment and ring for Polly to lock him in until the visitors arrived to question him.

The guest rooms, however, were singularly uncomfortable, and the food served on such occasions was spare and of an unusual taste and colour. The official interrogators rarely stayed long and returned less and less frequently.

Lord Scaith, too, was restless as news trickled into the glen and the Fortress of Glentarnock. He cursed the ineptness of his successor and deployed the lack of action in the world. He drank a great deal of malt whisky, fermenting like the malt itself. The spring had caused Polly to make herself a good tartan skirt.

Scaith eyed her as she served at table.

"Goat dressed as lamb."

"I lived in Albania once," Kuzminsky said dreamily. "Entirely surrounded by goats."

"Pass the dish to Mr. Kuzminsky," Scaith said.

"You'll pass the dish yourself," Polly snapped, set it on the table and flounced out, her tartan skirt swirling.

"Hoity-toity!"

Scaith helped himself and passed the stew.

"Goat?" enquired Kuzminsky.

They drank and passed the bottle. Lord Scaith mellowed.

"I have been thinking."

"Yes?"

"You know, those bloody Russkies are moving